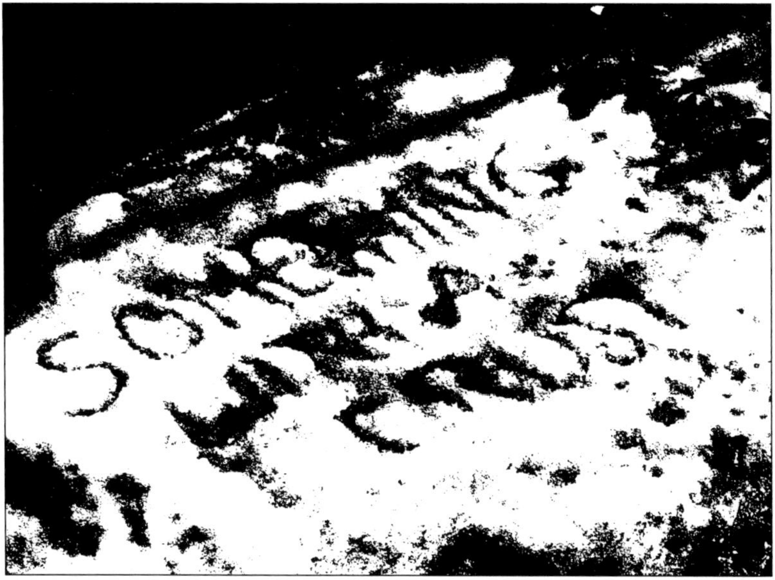

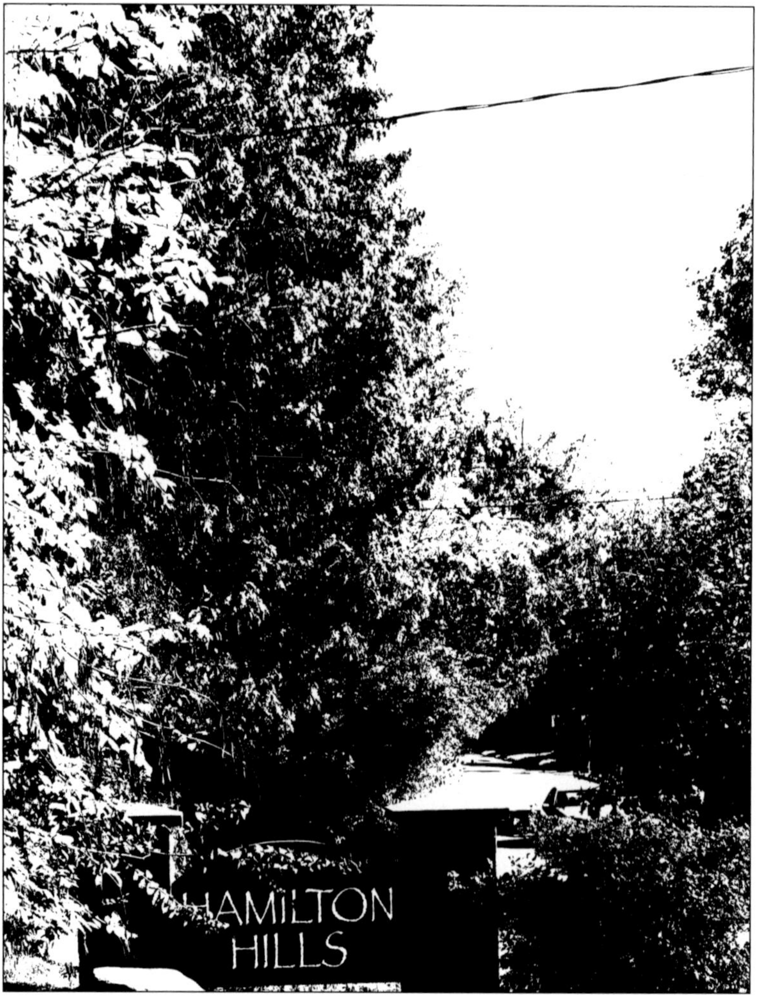
HAMILTON
HILLS

Something with a Crust

stories from Hamilton

Kimberley Lynne

Copyright © 2013 by Kimberley Lynne

Printed in the United States of America
First Edition

Lynne, Kimberley, 1961-
Something with a Crust
ISBN 978-0-9892562-0-9

All rights reserved. No part of this book may be reproduced or transmitted in any form or by any means, electronic or mechanical, including photocopy, recording or any information storage and retrieval system, without prior permission from the publisher (except by the reviewers who may quote brief passages).

Any resemblance between the characters in this book and any persons, living or dead, is a miracle.

The Guru of Harford Road and *Keys* were originally published in Baltimore Fishbowl, February and March 2013, respectively.

Published by Running Water Press
Baltimore, MD 21214

somethingwithacrust.wordpress.com

For my mother,
Susan Nancy Schuck Lynne

dear Charlie,

thanks for the order :)

enjoy the stories +

"hear a little further" as

Prospero would say :)

♡ 2 u + Kathy,

X.

Something with a Crust

10   Keys

16   Boxed in Love

22   A New Minefield

34   Baked

40   The Guru of Harford Road

44   Tree People

58   A Little Wilderness

62   Next Door

70   The Whim of the Great Magnet

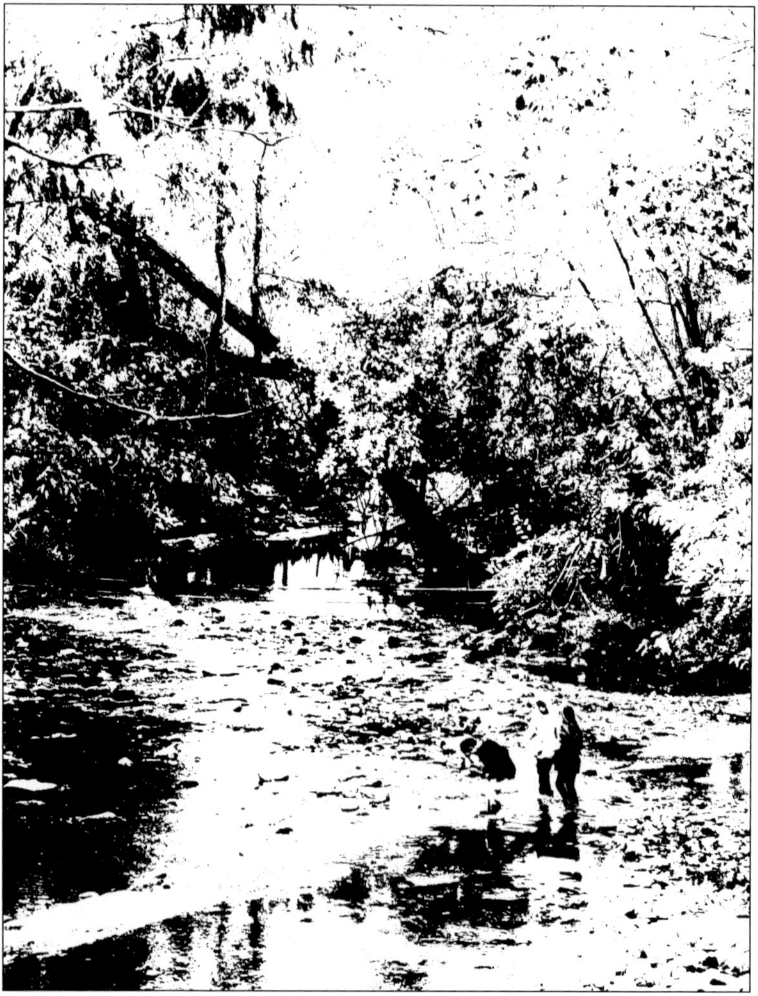

The stories of this neighborhood match its topographical history; the land was once wood and is still dotted with thick pockets of vegetative wildness that is mirrored in its inhabitants.

Hamilton has long been a little untamed, and many of its streets have forest names: Beechland, Fair Oaks, Glenmore, Evergreen, Woodbourne, Fleetwood, Pinewood, Sylvan and Hemlock.

My mother and her cousins are Hamilton girls. My memories of parties at my cousins' houses are smoky whisps of beery noise where women in high heels served pickled mushrooms and crabcakes.

"Oh, he's a Hamilton boy." I remember hearing in my teens about the wild young men who would swing from ropes off buildings, barbeque whole pigs in the backyard and race stockcars. Baltimore is swarming with individuals, but there must be a higher percentage in this neck of the woods.

When Hamiltonian writer and teacher Tony Reda returned me to the hood in my thirties, I fell in love with its architectural variety, its winding rabbit-warren streets, its rolling hills, and its lack of pretension. I bought property here because its eccentricities allow me to be the closest thing to me that I can be.

Or as Hamiltonian writer and designer Lauren Beck says of her beloved hood, "If you can't hang, get out."

Kimberly Lynne

Keys

"Don't I know you?" the Key Maker asks me. He's even shorter than I am and built like a fireplug. He needs a step stool to reach the key templates hanging over his workstation. He has stubby fingers and a halo of fine hair.

When I shake my head, my bottle cap earrings bounce against my neck. I'm wearing dangles, so I guess I don't really want to be invisible during these Saturday errands. Still, I'm glad my hair's unwashed and I'm wearing these baggy clothes; sometimes it's easier not to look pretty. I don't have the emotional fortitude for conversation; a sob lurks in the back of my throat, threatening to rise. The tired people who need key copies hover in some transitional zone between lovers or roommates; the Key Maker should respect our code of silence.

"Hey, I think we might be neighbors," he says, oblivious. "One street away." He compares my security door key to a series of metal templates.

This is Carl's fault. He dumped me and kept the keys. He might sneak into the house; I thought I heard him Wednesday night. I need to block him out; this time it's really over with him. Now that Ashley's living with me, I need to provide a more . . . consistent home for my niece. I can live in a man's orbit; she can't.

"Oh. Which way?" I ask, trying to divert the Key Maker from my house to his.

As the Key Maker lists our overlaps, I remember him. Every year at the end of May, he covers his rusted Gran Torino in movie posters and a hand–lettered sign wishing Clint Eastwood a happy birthday and rigs an American flag to a baseball bat wedged in the passenger window. He drives around the hood, honking his horn and waving, like he's running for office. The first time I saw this personal birthday parade, I stood glued to my lawn, staring at the gunfighter image from *High Plains Drifter*. (I've watched most of Eastwood's films with Carl, who loves a vigilante.) The gun and rope in Clint's hands made me feel both uneasy and secure.

The Key Maker further proves that we're neighbors. He works as a part–time postman; he says we've talked by my mailbox. He remembers that I work at Guitar Center. He and his wife live on Fair Oaks. I feel unexpectedly comfortable in that cozy bubble of shared niche; the world of Hamilton is thick with surprise.

"How much did you pay for your house?" the Key Maker asks.

I don't talk to boyfriends or family about money, but this troll of a man takes on the mantle of the anonymous bank manager. "I don't remember how much," I stutter. "Somewhere around seventy."

"I paid forty–five."

"Wow." That sounds cheap until I picture the corner house that I think is his, and it's worn with mold, time and dirt.

"Well, it's not in as good shape as yours," he says and pulls a lever down onto a vise. A squeal pierces the painfully bright store.

I look at the rows of shining keys. I don't like us thinking about our houses one street away, even if he is eccentric and probably harmless. A woman squeezes her shopping cart past me, making me shift closer to the Key Maker, near enough to smell his onion–scented sweat. I want to leave the store but can't face that awkward moment of requesting the return of my keys. Instead, I back up a few steps toward the screwdrivers and ask the Key Maker about his employee discount. I don't agree with the store's corporate politics and wonder how they treat their workers.

Key Maker ignores my question, and, as if he's been waiting to tell some local some juicy gossip, he asks if I heard "that screaming a while back in February." He croaks under the whirring grinder as if he was telling a ghost story. "It was as still as Christmas Eve, and we were bundled up in our bed when we heard shrieking like a banshee."

I nod. I've heard howling arguments in the intersection at four o'clock in the morning, the piercing sound of angry cries cutting through the calm, the skid of a racing car taking the corner, the scrape of fights in the street, gunshots.

That bitterly cold night Key Maker looked out his bedroom window to his front yard and found a woman covered in blood and wearing a torn slip, sitting in a snow bank. Her boyfriend had pushed her out of his truck and left her there, or so she claimed. Key Maker says she looked like the actress Sondra Locke: big–toothed, blonde and vulnerable. He seems wistful, describing the girl who was so skinny that her collarbones stuck out.

My mouth gapes. I forget the keys and the bustling store around us.

Key Maker and his wife wiped the girl off, put an old coat on her, and helped her into the back seat. Her parents lived nearby, but she said she didn't remember their address. She whimpered something about silverfish and bugs. Not knowing where he was going, Key Maker turned on the engine to warm it.

In the icebox of the car, they argued; she said he reminded her of her father and that was not a compliment. His wife lowered herself into the passenger seat and ordered him to drive, so Key Maker slowly started up Fair Oaks.

"So the girl's covered in blood," he says to me in the store, "blood coming outta her nose, he really beat her up, and she's sitting in my car, wearing my coat, and yelling about her father, and I say, look, I'm trying to drive here, and I don't even know where!" He's excited and waves his arms, certainly not with the cool reserve of Eastwood as The Stranger.

I can see the scene in my head: the screaming match in the car, bumping through mountains of snow.

A series of lies poured out of the girl slumped in the back seat, stories falling out of her mouth like white water. She said she was a pole dancer in a prostitution ring run by a firefighter in Hampden. Then something shifted, Key Maker says, and she switched accounts and said that she and her boyfriend were celebrating his release from jail in a bar in Parkville, "the one with the funny hat." Key Maker pauses for effect. She gagged a little, he says, and held her matted head in shaking hands. She murmured that she was from the Eastern Shore, and she had tripped on acid for the first time on Valentine's Day.

When Key Maker imitates her, he pitches his gravelly voice higher, so falsetto that it makes him cough. He says that the girl stopped making sense after that and muttered something about a clubhouse and checking for wires.

"She hurt, she said, you know, hurt, but she didn't want to go to the E.R." Back in the Tool Corral, Key Maker wrinkles his splotchy nose and tips up his protective goggles. His eyes are a pale blue under the film of cataract. I hope that he doesn't wink; he doesn't. He says that his wife thought that the girl had a headache from the beating.

I rub my forehead and frown. Last week, Carl shoved me down the stairs and swore it was an accident, but I felt the push, and my back still clenches. I wonder what I would do if I found a slip of a girl on my front lawn. How this quiet Sunday has shifted and swayed, when all I wanted was to get key copies, pick up some cable ties and then take Ashley to Dick's Sporting Goods to buy shin guards.

"We took that poor lost girl to her parents' house," says Key Maker. "I guess we should've taken her to Good Samaritan Hospital, but come to find out her parents live right on Hemlock Avenue, a little blue bungalow." He turns off the grinder and wipes his hands on his grimy apron. "I had to take her somewhere."

I open my mouth, but I don't say that the silverfish parent option was much better than the abusive boyfriend. The air smells of burning metal. I don't want the filings to enter my lungs, so I cover my face with my arm so I can breathe through the cotton of my Dead Kennedys tee shirt.

"It's a sad, sad, sad state of affairs," Key Maker says and sighs, polishing my new keys with a brush. "Sorry to bum you out." He smiles. He's missing a canine. "But that fireman stuff's true. They caught this firefighter running a cathouse with bedrooms and bars and hookers in Hampden, and he called it a clubhouse. That's what she called it in my car." He compares the new keys to the old one. "Gave her my old hunting jacket; it's too small for me now, and I didn't want it back all messy." He flips a key, trying the reverse of it. "I've seen her, you know. I won't say which one, but I seen her working at a local Royal Farms Store."

I can't lose the harrowing image of the blood–spattered blonde in the suburban snow. I wonder if Key Maker belongs to a neighborhood crime watch association. We have to rely upon each other when we live on the fringe of the Baltimore City war zones. We hunker down in our little castles and gather to shop and complain.

"It gets weird sometimes," I say, lowering my arm from my face. "I hear all sorts of stuff: helicopters overhead and electric saws and hammering at night. The house next door's been empty for a long time now, and I'm sure gangs use it."

It dawns on me that he's making copies of the keys to my house. He knows which house is mine. This doesn't seem like a good idea, despite his rescue story and the Eastwood parade. I shift my weight, curling my toes inside my sneakers. I wonder if Key Maker ever saw Carl go in and out of my house. I wonder if he knows that Ashley and I are alone there now.

He holds up the key to my wooden back door in front of his ruined nose. "I made the security door copies, but, sorry, we don't have this one in stock," he says, squinting. "It's too old."

Good, I think. "Thanks, neighbor," I say, taking the key envelope with two new security door keys and the back door key he couldn't copy. In the glaringly bright light of the Tool Corral, I search for signs: scratches, fingerprints, or cigarette burn scars. I only see eczema.

Boxed in Love

Frank soldiers up the Hamlet Avenue hill, his shoulders stooping and legs shaking through a low–lying cloud. A train whistles. His slippers slip on wet leaves; the ground is uneven. Dogs wake and bark; cars careen through the skinny streets, spraying pebbles. Frank's breath ruffles his moustache; he inhales deeply so oxygen will push away the argument rolling around his muddied head, but it doesn't work. His blood is still toxic, thickened and boiling.

He had bolted from the kitchen, seething. An ocean had tipped in his head.

"You shook a screw loose from the back door when you slammed it!" his wife Hannah called after him, her pitch rising an octave. "Do you hear?"

People in Bethany Beach hear you, he thought as he compulsively scratched the peeling rash on his arm.

"A screw loose!"

Did he imagine a giggle under her annoyance? Was she secretly gleeful when she yelled? In the upstairs bathroom, that morning, he had found a *Newsweek* folded over to a report on a psychological study that tracked female immune systems. The reporter claimed that wives become healthier when they piss off their husbands. Hannah had marked the page with several exclamation marks in red ink.

"Come back! There's water in our basement!" she screeched. There was no joke under that demand.

Drips make me feel at home, he thought, as he remembered the buckets in his parents' basement. They had skirmished about leaks, mostly to inspire each other to do something about them. Their fights had rolled like polka dances, violent but boxed inside love.

Frank had to leave the house. There was nowhere to hide when he and Hannah clashed. She followed him through the rooms and up the stairs, snapping at his heels like a sheepdog. He had never thought of his wife in a canine way, but suddenly her nose seems elongated, her eyes puppy brown, and her hair glossy. But, Hannah's mind is a girl's mind; she questions. She doesn't understand that when a pipe leaks, the solution is to turn off that pipe, not to call the plumber.

Determined to walk off his frustration, he continues his march up the Hamlet Avenue hill. At the top, he abruptly turns right on Hemlock Avenue, wondering about the robin's egg blue, clapboard bungalow where Ma had once lived. He stops and closes his eyes.

Years before Hannah, in the week when he had bought his house on Beechland Avenue, Frank had drawn a careful map to his new home for Ma, because she wasn't very good at directions. She only drove then because Pop had lost his right leg below the knee, and she wouldn't let him use that cane to depress the brake.

Two days after his property closing, Ma had quivered on Frank's back steps with empty bags and a broom. "I'm going to drive up Hemlock and see if I can find where I was a girl," she had whispered, enjoying the reveal that scared her son. "I think it's the third one." She had forgotten that first home until then; she had only been six or seven when they had moved north.

He wished she remembered history better. Even then, she was losing fragments of the order of her life, but she always saw reality a little differently.

Crows cawed. Frank imagined young Ma lying in her girlhood bed, clutching the sheets that she had lined with aluminum foil to protect her heart from radio waves. As a child, she was convinced that her heart would burst if she left the protection of a building, but she probably was inventing excuses to avoid the hike to St. Dominic's School. Toward the end of her life, she wouldn't leave her condo on bright days, because the sun activated a fuse in her head. She was either light-sensitive or a prophet, because she died of an aneurysm.

Thick clouds had hung on the horizon like cotton batting that day of Ma's reveal; they made Frank thirsty. "Your old home is that close?" His voice had betrayed him and cracked. He had twisted his moustache so tightly that chip crumbs shook out.

It was too late to sell. Although he hated to pay rent, the life–long commitment of purchasing property in his hometown freaked him out. He stayed in Baltimore only by default; his people lived here. He had bought in Hamilton because it was a safe distance from his parents' house, and he could walk to a dozen bars and the Harvest Fare Supermarket. He didn't expect to be able to walk to his genetic source. Somehow, completely by accident, he had managed to move into the part of the world where his mother had emerged. He was drawn by her blood to their heritage painted across the sidewalks and the oak leaves.

"Third bungalow, this side," Ma had said. She had held the end of the broom over her heart like a shield and teetered away.

Frank opens his eyes. Fresh from the Hannah Plumbing Fight, he stands before Ma's childhood home on Hemlock Avenue. Plastic flowers litter its garden and porch. A Blessed Virgin Mary on the half shell and a Little Dutch Boy statue guard the steps. Through the glass panel in the front door, Frank sees the tiny living room stuffed with bulging bags and stacks of magazines and newspapers. The shape of an armchair and a couch crouch under the hoarders' mounds of stained blankets and rumpled laundry. Figurines, tins, and candles crowd the shelves. Thin paths weave between layers of loose paper coating the carpet. A tower of empty pizza boxes teeters next to the TV. A matching tower of milk crates flanks the narrow steps. A flock of silverfish saunters out.

According to Ma, the house looked very much the same as it did in the fifties, and that gave her a sense of continuity. Frank's hoarder grandparents had a history of life on that Hamilton hill. Ma had learned to walk and talk in that house. In that house, she had first wrestled with the concept that words are paired with objects. In that house, she had learned consequences and had eaten homemade cookies. She had played under that willow tree when she was strong enough to face the backyard or wasn't strong enough to face her parents. (She didn't like the word *parent*.) His grandparents had divorced when she was a teenager, and Frank wondered if that ugliness took seed during those early years. They had slept together in that house, brushed their teeth, and taken baths. That energy was soaked into the walls, behind all the stuffed bears and vases, staining the plaster, their voices trapped forever, muffled ghosts pinned under the paint. The wall framing knew his grandmother's cries of passion and his mother's tantrums. Skin cells sprinkled across the caulking and the floorboards. Wood is porous.

Frank's stomach aches from the Hannah Plumbing Fight. He drinks vodka from his water bottle and fights the urge to knock on the hoarders' door. The buried room looks like his boyhood home, safe, and he suspects that the owners have few guests. He wonders if they have pets or kids; he hates cats as much as he hates the word *human*.

He runs a speech through his head, explaining to the current hoarders why he wants to see inside. "Ma was sad here. She curled in a basket in the kitchen for a week once. Of course, she was much smaller then. She got much smaller again before she died, and, well, I think she would've liked your candle collection."

Rain mists. Frank thinks that from the top of the Hemlock hill, he can see his life from a benign distance. He sniffs and wonders if Hannah can live without the basement bathroom. She never uses it. Maybe she wants everything to work, and that thought scares him the most. She was born in the land of plastic–coated sofas and weekly dustings. He shudders.

A car door shuts behind him. A ruffled curtain flutters in the side window. Frank hears sobbing under the flow of a shower. Several crows suddenly fly out of the willow tree.

Go home, he thinks. Go home and kiss Hannah before she coats the rugs with more sticky resentment and goes to work mad. Then she'll never make Sunday roast again or wiggle under you or say that you're her hero after you toss a spider out the door.

He likes it when she curls against him; she lowers his blood pressure then. In that calm, he can tell her most things. He tries to tell her the truth as he knows it, but he isn't too sure that he knows any truth at all. He feels awfully unworthy of Hannah most days in this first year of their marriage. He knows she doesn't feel that, but it doesn't help. He still sometimes feels like her pet and a not very well trained one at that.

Frank's bowels shift. Ironically, he has to return to the upstairs bathroom; it was inevitable. He pivots and walks back to Hamlet, trying to figure out how to fix the basement pipe without calling the plumber. His mother thought a plumber was a terrible waste of good money. He tries to remember the last time he used his unbalanced mother excuse for seemingly irrational behavior.

She lined my pillowcases with aluminum foil, he reminds himself as he slides down the hill, but she was only worried about the fuse in my head.

A New Minefield

"We're both musicians," Rance's sister Pru said at the monthly family dinner, picking at her chipped, puke green nail polish. She dug into a pile of olive tapenade with a flat bread spatula.

"That's like saying that a Great Dane and a Chihuahua are both dogs," Rance said. They hunched in the steak–scented twilight of The Oregon Grille, flanked by their chewing parents. Mother nibbled; Dad crunched.

"Which one are you?" Pru asked, rolling her heavily lined eyes. A waiter poured water at the adjacent table; the ice cubes clinked. Across the moneyed calm of the restaurant, someone opened a champagne bottle.

"You play the spoons, jerk girl," Rance accused.

"And other instruments. Cheer up, cranky," Pru said as she weighed her desert spoon, slapping it into her palm. "I'm playing a set and shooting the rest. C'mon, moody. The experimental music scene's huge in this town." His sister leaned into the candlelight and paused dramatically. "Dad's heard me."

"Are you trying to set me up with some spoon–playing girlfriend in hipster land?" Rance twirled his wine glass, thinking about wine legs and girl legs. "I hope she isn't like that blind date with the tuba player."

"I didn't know she was a dyke."

"Prudence, your language and your nails," Mother warned. The flutist of the family, Mother was very particular about everything. She plucked an errant hair from her linen pants.

"I'm not picking at my calluses," Pru said, overlapping Mother with justification. She and Rance needed their calluses; they played string instruments.

"Lesbians are great kissers," Dad sputtered underneath Pru's protestations, as he sprayed olive flecks on his silk tie. The family could talk simultaneously and still understand each other.

Pru laughed too loudly. Mother ignored Dad's comment by straightening the edge of the tablecloth.

Rance wiped his horn–rimmed glasses on his napkin; his left foot tapped on the carpet. "I'm cheered up," he insisted.

"You've hit a musical wall at thirty," Dad said to him. "Do you think maestro will put up with that much longer?" He rocked back and forth, tugging at the tablecloth. "Did we teach you nothing? Hear the chefs in the kitchen? That's music!" He sat still to listen to the distant cooking clangor and added softly, "You have to know the loss of love and the hole it leaves behind before you can fill it with art. You're blocking your emotions. Get your dick slapped some more, and then pick up the bow!" He flourished his butter knife, and butter flecks danced.

Mother cleared her throat and sipped her martini. Pru grinned.

Rance winced. He had heard the accusation of mechanical playing before; six months ago maestro had nicknamed him The Surgeon. The next week, the principal horn accused Rance of over–thinking. Maybe he had been focusing on the science of sound instead of letting himself feel. During concerts, he was distracted and convinced that he missed too many notes. Maybe he wasn't granted a sacred piece of family gift. An emptiness gaped in his music where an ache should ferment, but Rance hadn't let himself endure the angst of sentiment since his first love at band camp, Christy, who cared more about her clarinet scholarship than his wet kiss. He still longed for her, even though her lips were chapped and her hips wide. He tried to replace her with a string of clarinet–playing girls who teetered into the unstable, and as their neurotic, screaming fits flowered, his lovemaking grew as automatic as his playing.

Two weeks later, Rance stands in the light rain, searching for his sister and the Hamilton Arts Collective. He blocks out Christy thoughts by focusing on the street sounds: water trickles in storm drains and, across the street at the bus stop, a white bearded man in camouflage sneezes behind a newspaper. Some symphony friends call Hamilton's Main Street the new Hipsturbia of Baltimore, and Rance wonders how that label fits with the slim Asian woman in a round hat looping figure eights around the bus stop, holding up something like a magnifying glass. A quick, bright light seems to burst for a breath of a moment, like a gunshot flash but without the pop. Baltimore briefly rolls like a film, a dissociative cross between *Tin Men* and *The Seventh Seal*. Rance rubs his eyes, turns up his collar and checks his watch. An engine backfires. A few bars of Beethoven's *Sonata No. 2* run through his head, and the March drizzle patters along.

Pru will be easy to spot, Rance thinks; she's probably wearing something brightly polka–dotted like one of Dad's ties.

Dad must have experienced the loss of love; Rance never saw him caress Mother with passion. Still, the old man knows music, because inside his light touch of Beethoven lurk all the seasons of one human day. If the wheels weren't locked, all of his father's messy anger and remorse and joy would push the piano off the stage into the laps of the enraptured audience, and they wouldn't mind.

Over the Hamilton Avenue intersection, the sound of a mauled guitar shrieks, mixing with the mist, calling with formless, emotionally–charged beauty. Rance looks up. Across the street, a fire escape leads to a swinging door on the second floor where crimson light pours out along with the guitar screams. Paint chips off the doorframe. A split in the brick mortar crawls up the wall from the door to the roof. Rance's fingers twitch; they feel empty without his cello. He absently kneads his rough calluses.

A small, handwritten sign with two half notes, a bird silhouette, and an arrow points toward the open entrance of the Hamilton Arts Collective in the brick face of the corner row house. The door leads to a steep stairwell with shiny black walls. The stair treads are tagged with a series of pink bromides: *property is theft*, *workers unite*, *vote union*, *free education*.

Rance feels pulled by the siren's call of experimental music; his strides are bouncing and confident. Two floors up, the screeching bass builds and mixes with the low and haunting baseline of patchouli as he reaches an abandoned lobby where a disconnected gas range is the lone piece of furniture. On it, a clipboard with a mailing list sits beside an unprotected Cuban cigar box filled with a hundred and ten bucks. Rance can count piles of money by just looking at them. He excels at spatial relationships and is very good at packing leftovers. He thinks the cash is a mix of fives and ones.

Rance follows the squealing sound across the lobby. Beyond a beaded curtain at the end of the box office stove is the theatre. His pupils adjust, and he spies his sister taking photographs in the front row. She slouches and clicks. Rance scans again, and in this room twenty–five people sprawl on office chairs on risers. On a thrust stage, a wraith of a woman in a pasty nightgown wrestles with the microphone, singing about dark matter. Smudged triangles blacken her face from her sharp jaw line to her arched brows.

Cool air blows from the open fire escape door in the cracked theatre wall, the same door that allowed the music to spill onto Hamilton Avenue. In the front row, Pru shivers and turns. She waves at her brother; her flopping hand seems fleshy, like a starfish before it dries. She's wearing a plaid beret and a polka–dotted jacket. He crosses to her; no one in the audience seems to care if he walks in front of them.

He sits in a molded plastic chair beside her. "Hello, spoon player." He can speak in full voice and not interrupt the performance. A hole in Pru's bright orange stockings reveals a curly pattern. "Is that a tattoo?" Rance asks.

She taps her All Star Converse sneakers on the plank floor and pivots with the camera still blocking her face. She clicks Rance's flushed, damp scowl and turns to the performance.

The bass player wears a World War I helmet and worn football padding. The drummer wears some Middle Eastern head wrap in a leopard print. Rance can't tell the drummer's gender; he finds the androgyny intriguing. The lead singer howls and dances around the stage, her arms outstretched.

Rance wonders what Beethoven and Shostakovich would've thought of the frightening lack of musical structure; still its random lamentation aligns something clunky in his head. The pounding wave of sound fractures some block, like the crack in the brick on the building. His string–blistered fingers stop clasping his trousers. His face shines with wonder. He claps at the end of the set with the rest of the audience. The people seem as refreshed as his father's audiences, as if they'd woken from a long winter's nap. The band disperses; the evening is a series of sets. A pixie of a girl, not five feet of her and wearing a tutu over torn jeans and a pair of children's costume fairy wings, scurries about, switching microphones and re-plugging amps. Her once–rose tutu has worn to sepia with time, but it still sticks straight up when the girl bends.

He wonders if she's ever played the clarinet or any woodwind, really.

Pru hands Rance her Canon Rebel camera, distracting him from his Pixie thoughts. "Here," Pru instructs. "Photography makes me a better musician; it's a framing thing."

Rance shoots the Pixie and the band transition in all the different auto modes. "Portrait. Landscape. Close–up. Night Portrait. Full Auto," he says, listing them.

"You're Full Auto," Pru says, imitating an android by jerking her body, arms akimbo, her fingers rigid. He responds by photographing her. "Full Auto, you are the perfect son," she says in their childhood voice of the shrill robot.

He imitates her automatic cadence, but lowers his tone to harmonize with her soprano strain. "Night Portrait, you are jealous." He knows by her sincere frown that he's struck too close to sibling rivalry truth.

Pru drops their accent game. "Do you like playing or are you sucking up to Mother and Dad?" she asks calmly, like she's discussing the weather and not the family dynamic.

"Who died and made you shrink?" Rance asks. "I like playing cello," he mutters. He clicks the stage repeatedly without looking through the viewfinder. "But this so–called music stuff is crazy. It hurts my head, and thanks a lot for dragging me here. It's changed me as a person."

"You clapped. I saw you," Pru says. She spreads her arms to include the whole theatre and the artists milling around it. "I like this, this thing that's my version of Dad's concerts." When Rance doesn't respond, she flicks his carroty hair and sniffs. "Hey, you smell like lamb," she accuses, jabbing him in the ribs.

"You serious jerk girl, it's that rosemary shampoo you gave me."

The house lights flash. His sister takes her camera from Rance, apologizing. "Look, I'll be back, but stick around. I think you'll like the next one." She edges onstage with a handful of silverware and her camera bag.

Rance slumps and wonders if Mother knows about Pru's tattoo. He wonders if Pru ever plays percussion with other cutlery, like dangerous knives or forks.

The lights dim, and a normal–looking guy in a polo shirt walks onstage with a cello and a six–pack of National Bohemian beer cans. Rance straightens, interested. The polo–performer makes a big deal of opening two of the cans and chugging its contents. Belching, he wedges one can and then the other under the cello strings, right by the bridge.

Rance aches for the abused instrument, and he thinks of his at home: insured for more than his house, oiled every month, and re–glued every year.

The performer tears the bow over the cans. By lengthening the strings, he has changed the fundamental frequency, and the metal cans resonate in sharp, foreign, stinging wavelengths.

Rance drops his jaw, trying to pop his ears. He never knew the cello could make that terrible noise; he's shocked, as if he had discovered that his own heart made a racket it never had before.

The performer bears down so hard that he looks like he's carving a turkey. His straight hair swings like a mop as he saws. Horsehair hangs off the bow.

Rance tugs at his button–down shirt to scratch the tickle in his chest. Under the cello's cry, he thinks he hears the crack in his musical wall split with a horrifying snap. He grips his seat; he wants to rush the stage.

Next to the cello killer, Pru plays the spoons on her ginger thighs; the metal clatters. She drops her spoons and takes photographs of the audience. Some are stunned; some amused.

Feeling betrayed by Pru, Rance stands and solemnly marches to the back of the theatre, intent on leaving. He can't process the agonizing wave velocities of the butchered cello.

Above him, the mixer flashes, and Rance sees two young women sitting on a raised platform crowded with technical equipment. The Collective must be short-staffed; the women are running the show and the box office. He beckons to them. He wants to give them money because they've shown him something mysterious and sticky, a new minefield of harmonics and discordance.

The smaller of the girls, the Pixie in the tutu, bounces down a short ladder and pulls him into the dingy lobby. She's not wearing her wings. Her cropped hair is the color of tea roses and hugs her petal ears. She takes his ten dollar donation and thanks him on tiptoe. Her breath is moist, and she softly rolls her Rs. She smells vaguely of smoke.

"I'm not selling concessions now," she whispers into his neck and over the pain-laced howling, confused about what he wants. "But you can buy a Natty Boh at the end of this set." She smiles; her front teeth don't meet, and he can see her tongue.

He feels taller than his recorded 5'7". He steadies himself, blocking out the gnawing itch of the lamenting cello. He wonders if he could date a smoker who doesn't support capitalism. "Are you socialists?" he asks, pitching his voice lower than its usual Mickey Mouse tone.

The Pixie's pert nose wrinkles. She tilts her head like a sunflower heavy with seed. "Didn't you read the steps?" she replies.

Rance nonchalantly leans against the disconnected gas range; his fingers stick to its tacky surface. He tries to remember the pink slogans on the steps. "They're not very specific," he says. Sweat glows on his wide forehead.

"Oh, but they are, they speak to the illnesses of our country."

He focuses on the glimmering line of her Bjork–esque neck. The crying cello blocks words, so they fall out, jumbled and crooked. "Yes, please, Pru is my —"

"Oh, yeah, I like her pumpkin tights; they match your hair."

"Yes, please tell her that her brother Rance —"

"I saw you shooting me—"

"Has to leave," Rance finishes, and, then flatly, at a loss, he says, "I belong to the musicians' union." The cello dirge intensifies, so his knees buckle.

Pixie helps him into a crowded office off the lobby where he lands heavily on a piano bench. She removes a bottle of water from a cabinet, wets a washcloth with it, hands him the bottle, and pats the wet cloth against his neck.

"Baltimore Symphony," Rance explains. "My parents wanted a cellist. Pru plays viola. Sometimes we play duet. I'm more technically skilled, but she can convey emotion, and I've been . . . inside my head lately." He thinks he sounds like an idiot, but the cloth is so soothing that he doesn't care.

"Would you like a Valium?" Pixie asks.

"I'm on Beta–blockers," he says. "Thanks, though." He drinks from the water bottle and tries to find the right word to match the color of her eyes.

If I kiss her, he thinks, everything will change, like the five others before her. All possessive and needy, but, no, not this one, this one is her own. This one gets music. All shapes of it, but I don't know if I could listen to this every night or every week even.

Pixie interrupts his swirling thoughts. "My relatives don't play anything musical; they don't play anything but games," she says. "I got the Valium from them, so . . ." She trails off with her hand cupped on the top of his spine. "Lately, I guess I take care of people," she says and kisses the crown of his head, lightly, quickly, *col legno*.

His chest relaxes, and he breathes freely. She has kissed first. He's glad that he used the rosemary–scented shampoo. He realizes that the howling has ceased. The air becomes sharper and less particulate. He puts his hand over hers. His fingers tingle as hers curl inside his.

The cello killer bursts in, swinging his arms like an orangutan, knocking the door against a tattered wing back chair and carrying an open Natty Boh can. He seems taller in the confined room of mismatched furniture. "Oh, there you are," he says to Pixie.

"This is Carl," Pixie explains, withdrawing her hand and hiding the washcloth behind a beer carton. "He went to Peabody."

Rance rubs his calluses. "I got these at Juilliard and the BSO," he says. "Acting Assistant Principal. Cellist."

Carl burps in two octaves. "Smells funny in here. Like cooking," he says at the end of the last belch.

"I'm Dana," the Pixie continues, overlapping Carl's expulsions.

"It's my shampoo," Rance says. "My sister gave it to me. My sister who plays the spoons while you massacre a piece of art." In the silence that follows, he's aware of the mushroom smell of sex under the rosemary and wonders about the upholstered chair wedged beside him.

A strand of horsehair hangs on Carl's sleeve, remnants of the butchery. "I assume you graduated from Julliard," Carl finally says. "So, I assume you know that you have to know structure before you can break it." Beer froth decorates his knife–cut of a mouth. He slugs his Natty Boh and taps the can, assessing Rance.

Rance glares him down. "I assume you know that someday, someone might do to you what you did to that cello in there," he says carefully, breaking away from their staring game to nod toward the lobby and theatre beyond it.

Carl grins like a wolf baring his weapons. "Back off, professional, don't you worry about that cello. Destroying stuff can be very freeing. Sounds like you might need a little bit of that." He turns to Dana; her frilly left hip juts out at him. He fingers the hem of her tutu.

She edges away. "Get off," she warns him.

Rance wonders if Dana's lipstick marks his bald spot and rubs it, pretending to scratch. He hears water dripping somewhere. "Hey, the lady said to get away and when a lady says to get away—" he starts.

"The bow's not heartwood," Carl says, interrupting, his delivery clipped, low and ominous. "It's fiberglass; I got it used. It's a sacrifice!" That last declaration sounds like fighting words. He drums the Boh can in double time.

Rance rises; his fists ready. He feels the way he does when he practices in his underwear, dizzy and empowered. Then he hears Pru's barking chortle in the lobby. He realizes she's not laughing at him, but he suddenly understands Carl's comment about deconstructionism and feels foolish on top of a pressing urge to leave. Rance drops his arms, exhaling.

Carl backs against the office door, shutting it. "Are you shitting me?" he asks darkly. He clenches the beer can and its metal begins to crack.

Rance's stomach feels filled with coals. If he was home with his cello, he feels he could play her forever. If he doesn't play within an hour, his hands will wither and crust. He longs to hear in his cello's voice the summer days of his childhood, his father's passion, his mother's order, his first kiss with Christy, and the shimmering line of Dana's pixie neck. He longs to hold his cello in a hug, to stretch around her hourglass waist and brush her rough hair, to steady her with his knees. He knows now he can make her sing. He plucks the strand of shredded horsehair from Carl's arm and tucks it into the pocket of his Oxford shirt.

"I'm going home to play," Rance says very deliberately, breaking the tension. "I only practiced three hours today."

Dana opens the door and moves Carl aside, and he plops into the mushroom chair. His beer sloshes out of the can and into his lap. The gloomy lobby is empty again. Onstage, in the theatre, a new set has begun, and drums beat.

"How do you make a cellist play *fortissimo*?" Rance asks Carl as he squeezes to the door. It's the set–up to an old band camp joke: *how do you make a cellist play loudly?*

Carl gives Rance a filthy look. He knows the punch line: make the cellist play *espressivo* or with great expression. "So, I play loudly and with feeling," Carl says. "Some people like that, like your sister." He reaches for Dana's tutu again, and she again evades his hand.

Rance's heart hiccups at the sight of Dana's dodge. "Prudence can like whatever she wants," he states, covering his interest in Dana's hips. "And I didn't say I didn't like all of it." He smiles. "You're authentic, and you can improv; I'll give you that."

"Oh. Then, I'm glad you heard it," Dana says, her eyes the color of walnut, her waist the curve of his cello.

"You unlocked something. Thank you," Rance says. He feels an ache filling the well in his chest and draining into his arms; he's worried about the Pixie. Strains of the beginning of Shostakovich's *Symphony No. 7* run through his head, and for the first time he feels the pain behind it. "Love is dangerous because it will always end," he says sadly to Pixie, "and when Carl the Cello Killer leaves you —"

"He already has," she says. She backs Rance into the empty lobby, leaving the sputtering Carl behind them.

Rance doesn't care about saying goodbye to Pru, and he can't wait to tell Dad the news. The cello calls him, louder than the girl.

"Then, I will return," Rance announces solemnly and bows like a soloist before he pivots and heads for the slogan stairs.

Onstage, the roar of a chain saw starting up follows the trills of a harp and the whir of a blender.

Baked

Felix Tripman heard banging on his back door at ten o'clock at night. He had just swallowed a Valium with the last swig of lukewarm Natty Boh, brushed a mouse turd off his bedside table, turned off the lamp, and closed his eyes.

The wooden back door rattled. He pulled his bumpy pillow over his shaved head. His nephew, Minnow, was probably returning from his heroin runs. Felix refused to open the door or let him sleep on the sofa. Minnow could spend the night in that tent in the woods across the street with his junkie friends even if it was November. He had ruined all the spoons in the house and sold Felix's Led Zeppelin box sets.

Felix closed his eyes and tried to recall an afternoon in his youth when nothing was wrong, when Grandma Mimi baked and Grandpa Ralph watched the Orioles on Channel 13.

When Felix thought he heard glass breaking, he dragged himself up, lunged across the room, and locked his bedroom door. He suspected Minnow's customers. Even high, Minnow wouldn't break a window, but his junkie friends had loose ideas about personal property. Felix's laptop and the server were the only things worth stealing in the house, and they were in his bedroom, so he wedged a chair under the doorknob and returned to bed.

A dull clang reverberated distantly from the basement, and the valley outside echoed with crashes and calls through the darkness.

His mind wandered, and when he awoke, he doubted that he had even heard the glass break. Then he remembered that the carnival was camped at the Parkville American Legion Hall; maybe a carnie friend was hunting for some weed. He was drinking buddies with traveling carnies who used Brannan's Pub as a base, and he wasn't up to their late night shenanigans.

The Valium kicked in, and he dozed off again and dreamt of his mother in the kitchen. Mom–mom had been creeping into his dreams of late and usually frying bologna sandwiches when she did. Sometimes his Grandma Mimi would show up, and the women would bicker about what to make for dinner. When he was a kid, Felix helped them cut carrots and knead dough. His older and absent sister Theresa wasn't in any of those cooking dreams, but Grandpa Ralph usually barked from the living room for more Utz potato chips or another hot dog. When pots clanging and clanking pulled him from sleep, Felix thought Mom–mom might be downstairs until he remembered she was gone.

Maybe Minnow did break some glass. Felix opened his bedroom door and crept out. A floorboard creaked under him. Light bled up the twisting stairs. Someone was cooking in the kitchen, and, from the crash of it, the cook was heavy and not sober. It didn't sound like Minnow; he was lighter on his feet. The intruder clumped around more like Grandpa Ralph did, but Grandpa had never cooked anything when he was alive. He was a plumber and could barely boil water. When Felix heard the timer ding, he tensed, expecting an incendiary device of some kind. Nothing detonated, so he tiptoed back to his closet for his Little League baseball bat, but froze with indecision in the middle of his room until he had to sit down because he felt so dizzy.

When Felix smelled the warm flaky goodness of pot pie, he called the police. "But my nephew doesn't have a key anymore! . . . I thought I heard glass . . . And I can smell it. Someone's downstairs, cooking something with a crust," he whispered to the 911 dispatcher from his bedroom phone.

He remembered how he used to wait for his grandmother's apple pies to cool, breathing in their aroma. The buttery scent wafted through the uneven floorboards, mixing with his elevated stress level and tugging a memory at the front of his brain, an argument between his mother and grandmother. Maybe the baking smells were hallucinations, but he only had three beers, half a joint, and a sleeping pill.

More banging followed; this time on the front door. On the phone, Felix urged, "Tell them the back door's probably open! He, they broke in there!"

Felix gently laid the receiver on his comforter and crept downstairs with the baseball bat to meet the police. Still disoriented, he clung to the balustrade.

Although he had turned off the ancient television before he went to bed, it crackled with explosions. Sitting in Grandpa Ralph's recliner in the living room was a stranger in his late twenties, a mountainous man sporting Cleveland Brown boxers, a stained wife-beater, and mutton chops. He was eating a pot pie with a fork, and, if he was a traveling carnie, Felix didn't know him.

Outside, the policeman shouted Felix Tripman's name. The flashing lights of the cruiser danced across the floral wallpapered walls.

"Yes," said Felix weakly, responding to the cop. The seriousness of the situation hit him as he edged to the door with shaking knees. He had a baseball bat, but the intruder had a fork and was unpredictable, enormous, and only six feet away. "Coming," Felix barely spoke above a whisper.

"The A Team's on," the strange intruder said through a mouthful of food. A lone pea nestled in his hairy chest. "No spoons, though."

Felix watched him chew. "I smelled cooking," he finally said. "Is that pot pie?"

"Yup, thanks, creamy and salty," said the intruder. "Only heated in the oven. The microwave is the work of the Devil."

Despite the butterflies in his stomach and the grogginess of his brain, Felix agreed. "Better that way; the crust is crispier. Are you from the woods?" he asked. The police yelled and hammered. "Someone at the door," Felix said lamely. He unfastened the deadbolt.

"What woods?" asked the intruder pleasantly under the tumbling of cylinders.

The door swung wide, and cold air rushed in. A policeman stood on the front steps with one hand on his holstered gun and the other holding a flashlight. "Mr. Tripman?" he asked. "Did you call about an intruder?" He was slight but wiry and had very short, blonde hair.

Felix nodded and felt nauseated.

The policeman charged into the living room, pushing Felix aside and waving the flashlight. "Is that the intruder?"

Felix nodded again, clutching the doorjamb.

"Stand up and put the pot pie down!" the policeman bellowed at the intruder.

"I'm not done!" The intruder protested.

Felix tried to steady himself, but he lost his balance and slammed right into a radiator. When his temple clipped the hot metal, he heard a surprisingly piercing scream, and the living room went dark as he blacked out.

Felix thought he heard Mom–mom and Grandma Mimi fighting about Grandpa Ralph. Felix was hiding from them behind the recliner, and he seemed younger. His legs seemed shorter. He wondered if they were ghosts or if he was dreaming, but it really didn't matter. It was good to hear them again, and they sounded real.

His mother accused his grandmother of sprinkling his grandfather's dust over an apple tart. "What's Daddy's urn doing in the kitchen?"

"I miss the smell of him!" Grandma Mimi cried. Baked apple perfumed the house, tart and sweet.

"That's disgusting!" Mom–mom screamed. "Don't you dare wash that spoon!"

Crouching behind his grandfather's chair, young Felix didn't understand their fight and salivated at the thought of fresh apple tart.

"He was a plumber!" Grandma cried. "And now he's outside time!"

Felix could hear them struggle.

"Everything returns to the same stuff!" Grandma Mimi scolded. "Grow up."

Something big shifted in the recliner beside Felix, and he jumped.

When Felix re–gained consciousness, he had a terrible headache, and his lip was bleeding. He tasted blood. Red and blue light mixed into purple in the living room, and a siren keened outside.

Across the rug, the intruder lay trussed and handcuffed; he was crying about the uneaten half of the pot pie. "Crispy," he whimpered.

The young, wiry policeman overlapped the moaning, talking into his radio. "I don't think he knew the intruder, no," he said.

Other people entered the house and began all speaking at once. Someone yelled at the intruder to shut up. Someone else gently moved Felix's throbbing head into a neck brace.

Felix wondered what painkillers the doctor would prescribe. He wondered if he had ever ingested any of his grandfather's dust. That would explain his great love for Utz barbeque potato chips.

The Guru of
Harford Road

He is egg–headed. His skin is tanned, not a Creole shade, but more like grease that coats an abandoned order of breakfast potatoes. Time hasn't been kind to him. His missing sections of teeth give him a slight lisp. His thinning hair is combed over and peaked in the center of his skull, and something woolly grows out of his ears and wraps around the arms of his gunmetal glasses. His cheeks sag in pouches, pocked like pears teetering on the edge of decay. "I said I don't do battery," the lawn mower repairman slurs into one long word.

"This isn't the battery one," I try to explain. "This is the gas one, and I don't know how to turn it on." When he wouldn't fix my husband's old battery–powered mower, I had bought a second–hand gas one from him. When I couldn't find its oil dipstick, I returned to his crooked rows of engines guarding the parking lot beside his store.

The repairman's acolytes surround him, his greasy posse hanging out in their sacred clubhouse. Some work for him; some waste time. All their white chins are patched unevenly with scraggly tufts. The disciple in the frayed Lacoste shirt patrols the loading dock, back and forth, jutting forward his bumpy jaw. "You a teacher?" he asks me. "You look like one I used to have."

I wish I were a teacher, so I nod. Let them think that. Somehow that seems a better use to society than running the MRI machine at Good Samaritan Hospital. Thank goodness, he didn't ask for my name, I think, for it might change. No matter my husband Frank's absence, the grass continues to grow, and mowing feels like vacuuming outside. I wish I didn't have to deal with a lawn mower; that should be a man's job.

A haggard, younger helper, who is probably on methadone, twitches beside me, trying to be still, waiting for a command from the older repairman. His right hand clamps his shaking left one to his chest. "Battery like hum, like robot," he mutters. "Like to hum, like to hum, robot hum, hum, hum."

The repairman shushes Twitchy and picks his black–tipped nails. He tells me that he's a proud University of Baltimore alumnus; he knows his value.

I agree. The community needs him, this king of lawn mowers, this guru of little gas machines, this tender of American, status–driven engines. Homeowners must keep up with the Joneses. If the grass grows too high, people complain. Frank didn't understand that.

The lawn mower king tilts his hard–boiled head. Something mischievous and boyish rolls from one clouded brown eye to the other, lighting them like the end of his cigar. "You want us to train you?" he hisses happily, almost dancing.

I swallow and promise him cash in exchange.

He nods, shrugs, and wanders away across the lot, distracted by a dented pickup truck bouncing off Harford Road. *Lil Truck* is painted on its side and Ravens stickers cover its bumpers; it comes to a skidding stop.

The twitching methadone helper shows me the mower's oil cap, and we pour gasoline into the engine's mouth. I hear it gulp, refreshed. "Robot almost ready, ready, ready," Twitchy chants under his breath as he works. He pops beige gum. Threads of old bubbles twirl in his moustache.

"Maybe I'll name it Robot," I say, feeling sorry for him. I hear my vowels drift south into the nasal Baltimorean twang, so I'll somehow manage to fit into this fragile patriarch of oil–stained men.

Twitchy thinks for a minute, then removes the safety lock and demonstrates how to prime the machine. "Robot, dear robot, won't you come out and play? Dear robot, she loves this song." He sings new lyrics to an old Beatles tune. "Shiny. Push here," he explains.

From several feet above us, loading dock man watches, shaking his shaggy head. The lawn mower king listens to a tattooed and muscled biker as they carefully lift a mower out of the pickup truck. The acolytes smoke cigarettes and discuss the last Orioles game.

I have nothing to add about baseball. "You said robot," I whisper to Twitchy as I lean over the mower handle. The parking lot air sparks with something secretive.

"Pretend not to know," Twitchy spills in a rush. "He's working on something new, the king, something big. He sells that, and we can all live down the Severn and fish every day, even Mondays." He shakes with the anticipation or he fights tremors from heroin withdrawal.

Loading dock man appears at my elbow. "That's five bucks, teacher lady," he says, chuckling because I need instruction.

In the empty store, a shrill engine revs and catches; underneath is an odd ring of laughter. The king slowly turns to the dirty windows as a sapphire light flashes. Suddenly, I see the skeletons of old mowers hanging on oil–dappled walls, and then they disappear as the radiance fades. A plump ring of ivory smoke puffs out the back door.

"She at it again," mumbles Twitchy. "Doesn't like to be alone, dear robot."

More engines roar in a mechanical symphony; apparently no one alive has turned them on. "Crap," says loading dock man, limping toward the dock steps. "Minnow!" he calls over a sloping shoulder. "Get the Karo syrup!"

I shake my head, wondering how a machine can possibly run on Karo syrup.

Twitchy Minnow springs up from the lot and bounds to the store.

"What the hell?" the tattooed biker croaks. "Is this joint haunted?" He looks worried. "Because I'm outta here if it is." He heads back to *Lil Truck*.

The afternoon sun bounces off the lawn mower king's sloping forehead. His snarled eyebrows lower. He scribbles something into a tattered notebook.

Like mine, their shifting world is changing, and lawn mower ghosts are just the tip of the iceberg.

Tree People

Tony didn't want to park his rusting Civic in direct sunlight, because the baby squirrels in his shoebox on the passenger seat needed shade. He pulled over next to a house that was overwhelmed by a giant silver maple. Years of leaves clogged the gutters.

For the most part, Tony followed rules, so he didn't drive while he talked on the phone. His uncle's voice crackled in his cell phone; reception was spotty in the valley. Tony turned down National Public Radio. "Uncle Mark?" he called, but he only heard static.

He adjusted the beach towel that lined the squirrel bed so it too sheltered the three babies; they wrapped around each other like warm pretzels. Leaning his wiry frame out the window, Tony lit a cigarette; the crooked driver's seat creaked, and his black hair trailed down the door, as black as the entrance to a dream. Dead branches pocked a bitternut hickory in the adjacent yard. People should know that trees use energy to shake off their dead, he thought.

"Listen," his uncle Mark said in Tony's cell, his speech distorted. Uncle Mark started bad conversations with *listen*. "Can you . . . Lil Truck? The axle blew on Big Truck, and we got two trees . . . Manuel's over on . . . he can't speak a word of English, and you speak . . ."

Closing his eyes, Tony wished he could've stayed home in his trailer, shades drawn, quietly reading the June issue of *City Trees*. Every day, he thought, this sort of stuff goes on with Uncle Mark, out cutting trees with the crew. Something breaks or an accident happens right in front of him, like the elm branch last week that landed at Mark's feet and the chainsaw blade last month that snapped. Everything falls apart around him. Still, Tony liked the work. He liked healing trees, and he loved to climb.

"All right, so I shouldn't go over to Plymouth?" he asked into the phone.

"Go . . . stuck here at Pep Boys," said Uncle Mark, "and . . . stinks of tires." He said more, but his voice faded into the ether.

Tony blew a smoke ring and watched the breeze warp it. He turned to the shoebox. The baby squirrels' black–white–tan–speckled fur still stuck straight up, and their ears had just unfolded. He scratched one's head, and it sighed in its sleep. Then through his cell phone, Tony heard an audience applauding on the TV in the Pep Boys waiting room. "You know," he reminded his uncle, "I have the squirrels with me."

"Girl! I said girl! Glinda! I loaned the truck to this girl," Uncle Mark yelled into the phone over the TV.

Tony held his cell away from his ear.

"She's sweet," Uncle Mark said, describing the girl Glinda. "She rides the bus . . . public transportation in this town sucks. I met her at the Liquor Pump a week ago," he continued. "She was buying some . . . weird square bottle."

"You gave some girl Lil Truck?" Tony asked. Wait till I tell Pop, he thought, what his little brother did this week.

"Not gave. Loaned," Uncle Mark corrected him. He gave Tony her address.

Tony wrote it down on a Dunkin' Donuts bag with an old lipstick he found in the glove compartment. He considered the lipstick's owner and doubted that he believed in love after years of dating the wrong women who only inspired him to run. He stared at a quilt of winter creeper vine overtaking a forsythia bush.

Who names their kid Glinda? he wondered.

On the way out of Hamilton, he bought a Pepsi and microwaved the milk at the Royal Farms. The squirrel blog was very specific about milk temperature.

Back in the car, he aimed the plastic hypodermic carefully and squirted warmed milk into their mouths, and they purred like kittens. The largest one sucked on the smallest one's elbow, and the smallest one's ears twitched. Tony yawned with them as he tucked the beach towel around them. Then he drove slowly and grudgingly to the other side of Perring Parkway and into Baltimore County.

He thought that he should paper Glinda's street with *Tree People Tree Service* flyers. Hulking trees blocked out the morning sun. Stands of bamboo infiltrated yards. Glinda's row house sulked in the middle of a line of darkened and sagging ones. The lawn needed mowing. The roof was missing shingles. Tony parked his Civic next to Lil Truck; both ladders were still strapped to the truck's rack, and the trailer was still hitched. Tony considered hot–wiring it, so he wouldn't have to meet Glinda; his uncle's girlfriends were hardened, smart–ass types, but it wasn't always their fault that he dumped them after a month or so.

At the door, Tony held the milk bottle, took a deep breath and knocked. He knocked again. The door cracked, and a stream of perfumed air, spicy and exotic, escaped the vacuum of her house.

"Yes?" The voice was hesitant and husky, like a jazz singer who stopped singing because she might cry.

Tony identified himself.

Glinda was long and willowy. Her hair was a jumbled mass of rusty yarn, and her skin was the color of sun–baked sandstone or a swollen stream. She wore a big Orioles tee shirt and held a bottle of Amstel Light. She seemed too soft and pretty for his uncle.

"Well. Good to meet you," she said, disappearing into the cool.

Tony stepped in, as if he were walking onto glass or ice. His footsteps sounded very loud as his eyes adjusted to the dim of the living room that was furnished with a sofa, a TV, and a trio of wooden crates. Huge prints with wide swashes of color covered the walls. He tilted his head, trying to see mountains in the violet and emerald triangles. Something crashed in the back of the house. He heard her curse. "You all right?" he called.

She returned in a pair of torn jeans under the tee, rubbing her elbow. "Bumped it," she said. She looked at him with a look that made him stand up straight.

He smelled chocolate, maybe doughnuts, something sweet as she held out a Budweiser key ring. Her fingers were slender and two sported floral Band–Aids; each nail was a different shade of leafy green. Tony reached for the key, and as they held it together for a long moment, he thought he felt the metal vibrate. Close up, he could see the criss–cross of scrapes tattooing her skin.

"I'm a framer," she explained, watching his glance. "I frame art. It's hard on my hands." She nodded her head to the walls full of tree–coated mountains.

A bird sang plaintively in the yard. Shading the house, the bushes outside the front window swayed in the light breeze. Finally, Tony pulled the key into his hand, and the spell was broken. "I tape maps on my walls," he said. He admired the subtle curves of her hips.

"So you know where you are. I feel that," she said, turning. "You wanna drink?" she asked over her shoulder.

"No, thanks, but could you warm this up?"

She stopped on her way to the fridge.

Tony held out the water bottle half–full of milk and noticed that her bangs were cut at an angle. "It's for the baby squirrels," he said. "I found three of them in a tree we cut down yesterday. They're in the car. I put some Pedialyte in their milk to rehydrate them." She stared at him. "You hafta to feed them a lot and at a certain temperature. Somebody said call the Fish and Game department, because I'll have to release them eventually. I tried to talk to Uncle Mark about it, but he doesn't get it." He waited for her to react to the longest speech he had made in months.

She stood still in the middle of the kitchen. "That's sweet," she eventually said. The clock ticked. A motorcycle puttered outside. Glinda frowned. "Mark should get it." Her voice deepened.

"He doesn't. He goes through girlfriends, and he can get dangerous. Once, years ago, he was dumping a broken stove into Lake Montebello, and he capsized the canoe on top of his girlfriend's head." Tony handed her the milk bottle. "But that happened way before there was a fence around the lake, so you could sneak onto it at night." The microwave hummed, and Tony rocked on the soles of his work boots and tried not to look at Glinda's breasts. "He's kind of funny. I mean, he named the trucks those silly nicknames. Anyway, he seems a little . . . old for you." The timer bell dinged.

She handed him the heated milk. "I don't know why I'm telling you this, but I don't think it's serious," she admitted, tapping her finger on the counter and not looking him in the face. "I need Lil Truck. My Momma lives over in Northwood, and it's hard to get to her. You know, you hafta change buses, and they don't always run. She's been feeling poorly." Glinda drank a gulp of beer. "I'm glad you didn't say that he seems a little white for me."

"No, God, no, ma'am. No. Nope. No."

She waited, holding her breath. Finally, she said, "My Daddy's Irish."

"My Mom's Mexican," he replied.

She swallowed a smaller sip of beer. "Show me the squirrels," she said.

He led her to his Civic and moved the shoebox to the back seat where they sat on either side of it. Three baby squirrels curled around each other, their limbs linked, tucked under the towel. They spooned, and the largest one planted his paw firmly on the smallest one's head. "Fortunately," Tony said, "they had their fur when I found them, or I don't think they'd live."

"Look how big their feet are."

"I guess the rest of them will catch up."

Glinda filled the small syringe with milk. As Tony instructed her, she wrapped each squirrel in a towel and held it upright to nurse it. When she held the syringe against the smallest one's mouth, it pursed its pink lips and sucked. Glinda's eyes sparkled like the sun on Pilsner. "I had gerbils when I was a kid," she said, "and I had forgotten how we bottle–fed the babies."

Even though he was sitting in the backseat of his car, Tony felt as he did when he perched at the top of an enormous tree: his lungs full of oxygen, hyper–aware of the layering of sounds and the dimension of color. The world flowed by; he didn't care, even though he needed to meet Manuel and the rest of the crew over on Fair Oaks Avenue. He wondered if he should offer Glinda his Civic for the day. He felt bad about telling her the Lake Montebello stove story. He wished Uncle Mark had married his last girlfriend.

Tony leaned over the shoebox and lightly rested his forehead against Glinda's brow. He meant to whisper something, he didn't know what and he didn't know how, but only his breath came out.

She sighed. "Mark said you were something," she said. She bit her lip, pulled away and looked down the street, worried, like she had missed her bus.

"I'm sorry," Tony said. He played with the edge of the towel; the fabric stuck to his rough fingers. "You did a good job feeding them." When she tugged a twig out of his snarl of rebellious hair, he didn't wince. A coiled strand of it bounced and sprung back. "Thanks. Cutting trees is a messy business," he said. He shook his hair out and then clamped it back into its ponytail holder. "You should see us work."

"I want to see it. I like trees, the shape of them. I could help, maybe pick up branches," she suggested. She patted the squirrels, and Tony nodded. "I'll get some shoes and call in sick," Glinda said, and carefully left the car.

He watched her walk up the sidewalk to her porch. Her front door slammed.

"Oh, you mean right now," he muttered. He moved the squirrels to Lil Truck and waited. Kudzu vines choked an American beech next door. Tony felt a little like he might throw up. He clamped his jaw and felt the back of his neck for fever. He checked his teeth for strands of last night's barbeque dinner. The interior of Lil Truck smelled like confectioner's sugar, and there were additions to the front seat: a tissue box, a water bottle, and a waiter's corkscrew. Lil Truck was low on gas, and someone had programmed its radio to country western station WPOC. Tony sang along with Johnny Cash for a few stanzas. He felt far away from the neighborhood and right in the middle of it at the same time. He realized Uncle Mark would blow up this relationship like all the others. He realized he wanted to show Glinda the top of the world.

When she returned, wearing high tops decorated with rainbows, he said, "Put the beer down." She tilted her head. "I want you to be sober for what we're about to do," he said.

She put the half empty beer on the curb. "And what's that?"

He smiled. "How are you with heights?"

Tree People

"I never minded them," she said. She picked up the squirrel shoebox and climbed in the truck. "When I was a kid, I liked pulling myself across the top of the couch. I pretended it was a mountain ridge. I used to scale the fireplace mantle and the kitchen cabinets." She grinned at the babies. "Hi, little ones," she said. "I bet you've been to the top of a tree before."

An hour later, Tony, Manuel and the crew trimmed a towering magnolia on Fair Oaks Avenue. When Tony worked outside, he felt like a superman, wielding the chainsaw and dragging down limbs.

"The tree will be happier, now that it's pruned," he explained to Glinda. As the team cleaned up, Tony put her into a bright yellow harness that fit under her butt and crossed her breasts, and they climbed. "Put your foot in there and pull," he said, but he didn't have to instruct her. She clambered up the tree, even holding out the safety line so it wouldn't tangle. Her knees poked out of the holes in her jeans.

When Glinda and Tony stuck their heads out of the canopy, she glowed. "Oh, my," she said softly.

The morning neighborhood spread around them, bustling and alive. A man with frizzy hair walked two standard poodles. A dog barked. A Gran Torino trundled down Fair Oaks. Above the two-story houses, the boundless sky spread wide, and the bumpy carpet of tree tops rolled up the valley from Herring Run to Harford Road; the ends of the branches reached like fingers to the clouds. Birds swooped. Squirrels raced across cable lines. Glinda beamed at Tony, and he reflected that glow back, like he was watching a sunrise. He didn't want to speak; he thought it might get in the way of the big thing that was weaving between them.

Below, Manuel stood at the base of the magnolia and leaned against its smooth trunk, holding Glinda's safety line. He yelled in Spanish.

"*Ves mareado*," Tony interpreted for Glinda. "He says we look dizzy."

She threw out her arms and tipped her face to the sun. "We are!" She seemed to be gulping the air like she was thirsty. "I've never seen it all from here. It's so pretty," she said. "Almost like a postcard."

Her giggles sounded like tiny bells ringing.

"I have never showed a girl this," Tony blurted.

She lowered her arms and patted the wide, flat magnolia leaves that formed a skirt around her waist. She looked like an Egyptian queen. "Do you only want me because you think you can't have me or because you want me?" she asked him.

He didn't answer; he was still piecing that together.

She steadied herself in a crook of the tree. "I used to climb Daddy," she said, looking west toward Herring Run creek. "He was my jungle gym. He smelled of motor oil because he built stock cars. Then he disappeared, and Momma said we'd have to try to forget him."

Tony tried to imagine forgetting Pop. Suddenly, he wanted to protect Glinda from rejection, from buses, and from fathers who disappeared. He felt like he might be levitating, so he suggested returning to the yard. He had never felt unsteady in a tree before, and the crew had to get to the next job by midday.

When they descended to earth, Glinda grabbed Tony by his shirt and kissed him, hard but with no tongue. He longed to open his mouth and taste the sugar, but he tilted a little, losing his balance.

"The world was fine until you showed up," he said, unbuckling her harness. She smiled and steadied him.

By the truck, Manuel smirked and hooked his thumbs in his belt. Tony doubted that he recognized Glinda or would say anything to Uncle Mark, but still Tony called, "¡No le diga al Tio Mark!" Manuel made a face and walked around the side of Lil Truck to tighten the ladder straps. Tony hoped he hadn't offended him.

Glinda guessed the exchange's meaning. "Don't worry about it. I think Mark's dating somebody else besides me," she said, holding Tony's shoulder as she stepped out of the harness.

"Well, that's good news," he said. She was beginning to read him, and that made him feel safe to say hard things. "I don't mean to be mean about this," Tony said, "but why are, were you . . . dating him?"

She shrugged. "I don't know," she said. "There hasn't been anybody in a long time. I just didn't feel it."

"I know that. Scary that."

"Sometimes he makes me laugh."

"Lately I feel weirdly older than he is," Tony admitted. "Like we've flipped." Standing on the ground didn't make his dizziness go away. "And all this with you, well, that won't help." He took her bandaged hand. "C'mon."

They stopped at the same Royal Farms store on the way to the next job. Glinda microwaved the milk while Tony paid for their Gatorade, a pack of Double Mint gum, and a roll of Rolaids. Next to the cash register was a display of mood rings, ovals of sloshed color in simple cheap settings. Tony pulled one of them out of the display; it seemed to hum in his hand. It changed from black to blue–green to purple as quickly as he could blink.

"That all?" the cashier asked. She was blonde and frail with long teeth and a fresh scar across her chin.

"Yeah, thanks, we're not hungry," Tony said. Glinda nodded beside him. He held out the ring. "This fit you?" he asked her. She slipped it onto her finger. He picked a magnolia twig out of the bramble of her soft and springy hair.

In the silence that followed, Tracy Ullman sang *They Don't Know*.

"I've been trying to figure out how you two are alike, and all I can think is how you're different," Glinda said. "You stand with your hips centered. Mark likes a morning drink and wears leather. And your eyes are different; yours are brown like . . . and your hair . . ." Glinda looked down.

Tony's chest stung with heartburn. He shoved the Rolaids into a jean pocket and offered Glinda some gum.

The register rang. "Seven seventy–five," said the cashier softly.

Tony popped a stick of gum into his mouth and paid. He stared out the window at the blinding light shining on Lil Truck. Mile–a–Minute vine choked a wooden fence beside the dumpster. Like it or not, he had to talk to Uncle Mark.

Glinda leaned her forehead against his, and they breathed together. They were the same height. "Minty," she said.

Tony beamed. "Maybe we should buy something for him," he said. They looked around the store and wrinkled their noses. "Not in here. At the Liquor Pump." Glinda said the last two words with Tony.

When they left the store, they walked in tandem.

They settled back into Lil Truck, and Tony drove to the next Tree People job over on Woodbourne Avenue. He piloted the truck assuredly; he knew the secret ways through Hamilton and the potholes that dotted its streets.

"Do you like horror?" he asked her, grinning like a fool. "There's a new zombie one, have you heard of it?" They quoted the film's tag line together and laughed. "We should see it," Tony said. They swung past Big Bad Wolf's House of Barbeque through a cloud of smoked meat perfume. "Where I pick up dinner most nights," he said, changing the topic from movie dates. "It's one of the reasons I live here."

"I'm glad you live here," she murmured. She stopped braiding her hair and ran her finger along the tail of the smallest squirrel. It wriggled in response. "They don't mind my scent," she said.

"Me either," Tony said, suddenly remembering standing at the barbeque stand with Uncle Mark and Pop when he was barely tall enough to reach the counter. He veered the truck into the Harvest Fare Supermarket parking lot. At the end of the lot, a valiant staghorn sumac fought encroaching honeysuckle. Tony stopped the engine. "No matter how obnoxious he is or how he treats girlfriends, he's family. I don't want to hurt him." Tony felt awkward, like he was standing against a wall at a teen mixer, but once he spoke his anxiety out loud, he worried less about Uncle Mark, and something lifted.

"We tell him together. That'll be easier." Glinda leaned over the shoebox and whispered to the baby squirrels, burying her nose into their fur. "We'll say that we caught something, you know, like how you catch the flu or a cold." The largest one sucked on her fingertip. "It takes over, and ruins everything."

Gulls circled the lot. Tony muttered some Johnny Cash lyrics and threw the truck into gear. "O.K.," he said. He checked the mirrors. "But we have to stop at the Liquor Pump first."

She unbuckled her seat belt and scooted across the truck bench seat so their legs touched. He put his arm around her. "This flu stuff's messy," she said, twisting the mood ring off her left hand. "I can't wear it on that one now. The one before Mark gave me one of these and then wanted it back." She put the ring on her right hand and admired it.

"Glinda," he said. Saying her name made his mouth tingle. They drove in silence for several blocks. Ever since the tree kiss, they hovered in a close orbit as if their bodies held each other in an oval of gravity.

She flexed her scratched fingers and adjusted one of the green Band–Aids. "I don't care if I'm completely covered in scrapes with you. I usually do. Care."

"I care that you have scrapes." Tony held onto her sleeve; he had goose bumps. "This feels different," he said. He hadn't felt the urge to run all day. Somehow Glinda made the dark emotional buttons of family seem smaller.

"I can drink," she warned. She sounded serious.

"You can also climb," he said, driving Lil Truck through a curve. "I used to climb out of my high chair." Then, out of nowhere, he felt the urge to run; it started with contractions in his thighs and calves. Glinda barely put her hand on his arm, but her touch anchored him; she tethered him back to the world. He breathed in her confectioner's scent. "Maybe I can tell Uncle Mark that I'll work other jobs for a week while we all get this into our heads," he said.

"Maybe," Glinda said. "It's only been a couple of dates with him, and I think he's been seeing a stylist over in Rosedale." A gust of wind rustled a chunk of her unruly hair; she tucked it back into its braid. "I'm not in it for Lil Truck," she said. "I want you to know that. I was in it for the wheels with him a little. I'm not with you."

Tony navigated around a road crater, and the trailer rattled. He leaned over to kiss the end of her nose. Even the weirdest and most uncomfortable scenes in his head with his family didn't seem so frightening with her beside him.

She grasped the squirrel box. "You all right?"

"Yeah, good, but a little scared. Alive." He kissed her again, lightly, this time on the lips. "You know what? Your living room's too cold for these babies," he said, nodding to the squirrels in her lap. "We gotta find them a warmer place." He down shifted, and Lil Truck rumbled like an outboard motor. "We might have to trim back some growth from your first floor windows, and let in some light," he said. He took a deep breath; it felt good to break some rules.

A week later, on Saturday, Glinda and Tony drive to the licensed Fish and Game rehabber who would train the baby squirrels how to be wild again. Glinda holds a portable gerbil cage that contains the three squirrels; they've put on weight and are much more active than their shoebox days. They wrestle and hurl themselves against the metal bars, hissing.

"We can't keep them in the backyard," Tony says. "There're laws, and they'll be destructive in a few months, peeing on everything, attacking." He fiddles with the radio. "The sooner the better, so we don't get more attached to them."

"I don't like the word *rehabber*," Glinda says. She points to a gangly pedestrian with a bushy beard crossing Harford Road. "People in the street," she says.

Tony frowns and swerves his Civic; it has just rained, and the air smells of ozone. "People should be afraid of moving cars."

"What are you afraid of?" Glinda asks.

He's silent for a moment, thinking. "I'm not going to bullshit you. I've been with a lot of women, and I only let them in this far." He holds his hands about a foot apart and steers with his knees. "Because I figure once they get inside, they're not gonna find anything to hold onto." He didn't know that he could speak like that. He's startled by the brightness of his eyes in the rearview mirror. He feels like he can tell her anything.

She turns to him and listens intently. "You have plenty to hold onto," she begins until one of the squirrels nips her finger. "Ouch! The big one's teeth are coming in," she says. She examines her hand. "It didn't break the skin."

She's unchained his tongue. "I told you about Susie who up and left after two years," he quietly says. "Said I wasn't . . . motivated. And after that and before this, a bartender, Carla, more off than on, and that stopped last month, because it didn't mean anything to me and that scared me." He finished the last sentence in a rush.

"I'm afraid of wanting a beer buzz for breakfast," Glinda says, shaking her head as if to shake that desire out of her brain. The squirrels yap in their cage.

Tony kisses her nipped finger. "You didn't have one all this week," he says.

She frowns at the main street of Hamilton. "You haven't been smoking," she says.

He holds her hand to his cheek. All the words that had been waiting gush out. "I own this car," he says. "And my trailer. I still talk to my Mamá and Pop; they live over there on Echodale. I finished high school and two years at community college, but I like what I'm doing now and no girl ever got that." Tony has no idea how long whatever they have will last, and he doesn't care. He knows he can live and work and love in this neighborhood and never has to leave it. His heart feels bigger and oddly uncomfortable in his chest.

"I'm not a lot of trouble, now that Mark has stopped yelling at us," she says softly, taking her hand back to twist her mood ring and watching it turn from bright blue to violet.

A Little Wilderness

The morning holds me in its bright and windy arms. The light is so sharp that it cuts the fine hairs on my chin. The air is so clear that I wonder what is real and what is not. The dead at my feet are very real. I lean over, my back stretching, to pick up a branch cut by the hapless Baltimore Gas & Electric tree killers. The cut is uneven and torn.

A scraggly man with a facial tic pushes a lawn mower down Beechland Avenue; it clatters. He balances a gas can on a stick on his shoulder. An African–American man in his twenties follows him, smile clenched, strutting down the street, his jaw twisting a blue pacifier in his mouth.

"You a grandmother?" my neighbor Mrs. Webb calls from across the street. Her matriarchal voice rings over the macadam. Her house perches on a lot as misshapen as mine on a small pile of earth at the bottom of the valley. I think her daughters and their sons live with her. One daughter has spent time in Sheppard and Enoch Pratt Psychiatric Hospital; she told me that when she asked me for money once. The other daughter, taller with a bigger Afro and no wedding ring, helped me move the broken dryer that someone threw into my front yard. I first spoke with Mrs. Webb on the day my house was robbed for the second time. We bonded in the middle of that hysteria and truth–telling.

I hold the tree remains. The sap stains my gardening gloves. "No," I reply. I am not a grandmother, but several of my early friends have achieved that unsettling role. I still feel thirty inside except for my ligaments and tendons. They tell better time than my half–century heart.

"Then you don't have to buy Easter baskets," Mrs. Webb says, nodding. "I sent baskets to all eight of mine." She sits on her steps, tapping her cell phone against her Spandex–encased leg. She squints at the clouds crossing the sun. "I don't want to start cooking, too early. I cook all the time, for work." Her wig rests on her head crookedly, so curls crowd her thick eyebrows.

I stuff branches into their plastic bag tomb. They fight back, unfolding, their leaves curling. One branch nearly pokes me in the eye. The kiss of the junk tree blotches my pale skin.

"I am bored, so bored, bored, but I don't want to start cooking. All that cutting." Mrs. Webb takes a deep breath. "No one helps me, no one, 'cept my one grandson and he's no help." She examines her toes in her flip–flops.

Cooking's on my agenda too, but my other neighbor, a middle–school teacher with a compulsive father, keeps criticizing my less–than–obsessive yard work. I like a little wilderness in my yard and don't trim as neatly as they do. I keep the wild barely at bay, a reminder of the tangle inside each of us.

"Did you go to church?" asked Mrs. Webb. "My four–year–old grandson did."

I stop sweeping and lean on my broom. The optical illusion of the Air Force blue sky overwhelms me. I breathe in hyacinth. "It's so beautiful out here that the whole place feels like a church."

That shuts her up. She taps her phone.

I leave her and seek sanctuary in my fenced backyard where butterflies and bees swoop and lavender and rosemary perfume the air. The crickets chirp under the lemon balm as I collect a green harvest of pepper and thyme. Some atmospheric front marches toward me; clouds gather.

I think of one of my favorite Baltimorean expressions: *if you don't like the weather, wait fifteen minutes.*

I weed and trim in the yard and sit on the back steps when I have to take a breather. Single quiet drops fall out of a lowering sky. The sand flies bite me through my khaki pants.

Suddenly, Mrs. Webb's screams rise and fall inside her teetering house. I can't make out the problem, but someone has done something dreadfully wrong in the kitchen, something about the ham. A helicopter rolls by. Someone up the street turns on a table saw. Then the sound of tech club music floats on top of all the other neighborhood sounds, soaring, matching the argument, eventually overtaking and melding with it, like opera. I stand and walk around the end of my fence.

In the driveway, Mrs. Webb's grandsons are seat–dancing in a parked Toyota, listening to the radio, waving their arms, blocking out the fury. They are around seven or eight years old and are perpetually moving like puppies. But they never will block out all that fury. They will carry pieces of that wilderness with them into every bed; carry with them the ghost of that voice in the kitchen.

Sweat runs down my back. Storm's coming soon. Something that sounds like a large piece of metal landing in a dumpster rattles up the hill. I breathe in the fresh rain. Thunder grumbles a few streets west of me.

The birds chirp, "Water, water, water!"

Two white male junkies push a baby carriage down Hamlet Avenue, but there's no baby in the carriage, only bulging plastic bags decorated with bright yellow, smiley faces.

Next Door

Some nights the helicopters circle, and the sirens wail. Some nights Dana comes home to the whine of power tools and even lawn mowers at midnight, but on this night no table saw hum breaks the soft ring of silence. The valley waits so quietly that Dana can hear a faint scratching inside her bedroom wall. She shrinks into herself, tightening, glancing toward a dust–mottled baseboard. She likes her home world dim; her cluttered bedroom is lit only by the bottle–green glow of *Spider Solitaire*. It doesn't matter if Dana wins or loses the video card game; she only wants to sort. She doesn't want to think about how to pay Ashley's tuition when the trust runs out; that thought makes her stomach drop into her sweat pants. In the adjacent bedroom, her niece snores, and Dana hopes she hasn't inherited her grandmother's deviated septum or her mother's bossy tone.

A light flickers in the second floor of the abandoned house next door. Dana turns her pixie profile, and her open window lets in the scent of magnolia blooms, rotten and lush. For two years, the house next door has been empty except for the mice and a foot of water. A crooked message about *bitch suckin sumfhng* is spray painted on a window screen; Dana can't decipher the last word. In the abandoned backyard, ivy reaches over mysteriously–shaped plastic bags, moldy plywood chunks, broken radiators and rejected furniture. Junk trees replace fence posts. In the summer, puddles breed mosquitoes, and the grass sways hip–high. Empty chip bags cower in corners and rest. The basement door gapes open, and rats travel in and out.

Still, the candlelight pulses. Dana runs her nicotine–tainted fingers through her auburn hair. She plays the Jack of Hearts on the Queen of Spades; each decision narrows the next possibility.

Default is always a possibility. "Baltimore's full of dead houses like this," said the realtor listed on Theresa's foreclosure notice. His singsong voice crackled on the phone at Dana. "The banks and the courts fight over 'em." The lack of care in that statement made Dana's spine rise as if she had been pushed into a corner.

Dana had filed a complaint about the trash piles, but garbage doesn't exist to the city unless it's blocking an alley. One hot morning, she had moved some of the crumbling plywood and the dripping bags, but she feared ticks and snakes. Vines choked Theresa's cracked TV set and three-legged deck chair. Dana felt oddly watched, as if the house had eyes. Her gloved hands were black with some nasty ooze, and, as she sifted through the layers of broken CDs and videocassettes, she peeled back the inside of Theresa's nights. She didn't want to know what movies her ex–neighbor liked.

They used to talk over the fence, sipping coffee and complaining about wet basements and high taxes. Theresa used to say that her house would wear her out one day; taking care of it was so expensive. Something was always falling apart. The basement, the porch and the garage roof all leaked. Dana would bite her lip and say nothing.

Then, Theresa vanished. There was no moving truck and no stacks of boxes on the lawn. She had probably snuck out sometime around Halloween; a cardboard ghost haunted her locked front door, mocking Dana, reminding Dana in her dead sister Rebecca's bossy tone, "You live one month behind all your bills too." That accusation was part of the last conversation Dana had had with her sister; a bus had slammed Rebecca and her embezzling husband on their way to the cleaners. Dana's pill–popping parents couldn't care for Ashley, so Dana's niece moved in with her, her niece who was accustomed to soccer lessons and private school.

Then the wind blew the ghost off Theresa's front door.

The flickering light in the empty house distracts Dana; she wants to close the blinds. Whoever is in there is in there illegally, and she doesn't want some gang member to see her through the magnolia branches. Years before, when Dana's house had been robbed, the cops had called it a case of gang–related initiation. All her dresser drawers had been turned upside down. They were looking for Game Boys and diamond jewelry, things they could fence. Dana was grateful she wasn't home at the time and doesn't want the possibility of another robbery with Ashley the latchkey kid around.

Rebecca had once said that another gang initiation rite was *riding train*, a bad expression for the rape of one girl by a group of boys in an abandoned house. Her sister had said that she had learned the term at some sort of work training.

Girls usually don't get raped in Rebecca's old neighborhood unless they do something really stupid, Dana thinks. At her bedroom window, she reaches for the blinds cord; she'll just block out the light.

A girl suddenly screams, "No, no, not, no, don't, I won't tell —" Her voice squeaks and is suddenly muffled like a cornered mouse.

Dana's hand clenches; she can't tell the scream's source in the neighborhood's little bowl of a valley. A tense silence follows the screech; the sound slit the night's ceiling with such sharpness that Dana thinks she can hear the stars flap. Adrenaline rushes to her heart. She tastes blood where she bit her lip. She listens intently, but all she hears is the cricket baseline of the night.

If I call the cops, she thinks, the gang will somehow know. They'll come looking for us. They know where we live. They stole my laptop. We're the end house.

A cat plaintively calls in the maze of pachysandra below; they fight and mate in the ground cover. A car lumbers by, rattling over potholes. Dana closes her eyes to listen harder for signs of human struggle. She remembers a story another neighbor had told her about finding a bleeding woman in his front yard in February. The city can be suddenly violent.

Dana flashes on the claustrophobic pressure of being pinned under the cop with the melon–ball breath in the SUV Minivan in the woods of Robert E. Lee Park. Something had changed in their kissing that night long ago, something she couldn't control. What if somebody had heard her in the middle of that night?

"Aunt Dana?" Ashley's awake; she's been having nightmares. Dana goes to her and buries her pursed lips in her niece's fine hair. Dana lies to her, assuring her that the girl's yell was part of her bad dream. Ashley looks skeptical. "Are you in tonight?" the child asks.

Dana has changed her old late night habits; she stays home most nights and only works Sunday shows at the Hamilton Arts Collective and mostly to meet that nice cellist. "Sure, but I might smoke on the porch," she says, tucking the blanket around the little girl version of her lost sister: skinny, stubborn, and slightly judgmental. Dana looks for her brother–in–law in her niece's face but can only see her straight-laced sister at ten.

"Shouldn't smoke," Ashley mutters and drifts off again.

A person's views change with the arrival of a child. Now, in the middle of the night, Dana tells herself that crap alone in bed, the stuff that Rebecca used to say to her: don't smoke, don't go out late, and don't sleep around. Dana stares at her niece, marveling how old she is inside. She feels like she has to catch up to her. The streetlamp's glow filters through the dirty blinds and crosses Ashley's curved cheeks. When a frown ripples Ashley's forehead, Dana reaches to smooth it.

A repeated banging from the house next door thumps like an angry pulse of a headache, so Dana creeps downstairs to check ground level. The night is waiting. The darkened living room smells vaguely of melon drenched in lemon and gin. Fleshy and cloying, it sticks to her translucent skin. She wipes her arms absently.

Just check the porch.

She puts on her navy pea coat, her snow boots and her ex–boyfriend Carl's old woolen hat. She pockets a Swiss Army knife and a flashlight. The sweet soup of Carl's sweat stains his hat and briefly overwhelms the living room melon. Dana thinks about his long–legged walk and something catches in the back of her mouth. Angry, she shakes away her vaginal need for him. She tells herself that she should be thinking about that nice cellist who keeps showing up at the Collective and not heartless and orbiting Carl.

She turns off the back porch light, unlocks the kitchen security door, and slides outside. The May air is surprisingly cool. She hunkers down in her coat, tucking in her shoulders, and locks Ashley in her house. She eases down the steps into the mysterious backyard of night. The earth gives under her boots. The moon seems ominously closer and bigger. The thump next door is replaced by a clatter. A dog barks up the street, and Dana kneels in the damp, shaking. Her pale hands glow. She scoops up a handful of the potting soil that she had spread around the lemon verbena that afternoon, and she rubs the dirt over her freckled cheeks, keeping it clear from the edges of her eyes. The dirt mask straightens her shoulders. Each breath smells of her land. She blinks, and light sparkles in the upstairs window next door. She inches to the edge of her property, stopped by the scrape of Theresa's old back door. Two hooded boys step into the night, checking the backyard perimeter and adjusting their jeans. Dana presses her gritty face into the wet grass. She hears the boys skip lightly down the steps and hurry past the overgrown garden thick with radiators and tires. The grass hugs their thighs.

    Breathing in the musk of the earth, Dana thinks of the times when Carl used to screw her airborne; she would fly over him, connected to the planet only through him. She doesn't know what kind of sounds came out of her body then. Maybe the scream she heard at the bedroom window was that kind of scream. She can't make those sounds in the house anymore, not with Ashley down the hall, not that Carl is around to carry Dana to that dizzy noise. She feels like a once favorite dress left to languish in a crowded closet, close and pressed and yet not wanting to leave, both lonely and relieved. She has no Carl story clean enough to tell Ashley. He pushed her down the basement stairs; she's changed the house keys.

    A car drives off, screeching down Roselawn Avenue, cutting into the fabric of the night like the girl's cry. Dana knows that the scream she heard at her bedroom window was a pinned–under–a–cop, melon–ball kind of scream.

    Dana crawls over the fallen fence; her unprotected fingers reach blindly. She ducks behind a shifting stack of leaking trash bags; gone from her racing mind is the threat of ticks or snakes. Theresa's old back door opens again, and two more boys gallop across the yard. They're sidetracked by a helicopter swooping through the starry sky and slicing neighborhood sleep cycles like the scream. The boys duck the helicopter's scanning pool as they dash for the street. Dana runs up the porch steps, and, before she can think any further, she opens the door and slips into the dank kitchen. She snaps open her knife.

The house stinks of shit. Wallpaper's ripped. The sink's missing, and the pipes have been cut to the walls. Graffiti's sprayed on the cabinets; spray paint cans cover the counter. The fridge door sways open, dripping. Something scuttles down the hall, and something above whimpers.

Don't breathe.

She closes her eyes and pictures inside the cop bar and the mustached policeman in the Ravens tee shirt, leaning over the smoky pool table with the jukebox behind him and the lizard–green drink beside him. He smiled at her, and she felt so pretty. The prettiness slunk up her spine and clouded the front of her brain.

She opens her eyes and aims the flashlight down. Syringes, spoons, mice poop, and pacifiers litter the wet and jagged linoleum. She gags from the stench of piss and vomit. One hand clamped over her mouth, she runs upstairs; the floorboards creak under her, and she slips near the top.

In the smaller of the two bedrooms, a red–haired teenage girl lies bound beside beer bottles and a sputtering candle on a plastic saucer. Crying has moistened the girl's turned–up nose, and her green eyes are glassy with something distant. Her cream camisole is torn, and she shivers in her leather jacket. Dana recognizes her from the pack of kids who promenade on their way to school at the Friendship Academy of Engineering Technology, all talking at once and shedding Coke cans and Tastykake wrappers. A tattered pink hair ribbon is spread carefully in a fan on the cigarette–burnt carpet, almost like a prize.

Dana looks away and through the magnolia, the opposite way to her house and to her murky underwater bedroom light. How different and far away the world looks from another house, almost safe.

The bound girl squeaks indignantly. Dana removes the soiled athletic sock from the teenager's cherry mouth, and the girl spits. "Your face," she says.

Dana rubs the lawn from her cheeks and untangles the bungee cord from the girl's ankles and wrists, leaving behind soft ditches that the girl kneads. She adjusts her tarnished bronze anklet that reads: *Pookie*. She fixes her feather earrings and applies fresh lipstick.

"Do you know them?" Dana asks of the girl's rapists.

The girl stands up too quickly and buckles. Dana steadies her, and a cloud of lavender and mushroom soup sweat blocks out the sharp sting of urine.

"They can't take anything from you, really," whispers Dana as they limp down the stairs, her arm snug under the girl's swampy armpit. "You're still you," she says, her back clenching. Pushing out of the kitchen, they escape the potential tomb of the empty house. The porch and the backyard seem clear until the helicopter whacks overhead again. Dana's stomach contracts as she breathes clean air. The moon tips.

Pookie pulls away and checks her pockets. "Gotta go," the girl announces under the smack of the helicopter blades.

"Do you want to go to my house, next door, and clean up first?" Dana asks, but the girl ambles down the steps, removing a cell phone from her fringed leather jacket. Dana whispers, "Pookie." The sound catches in her throat and tickles. "We forgot the candle upstairs."

"I can't go back there," Pookie says. "Ever." She pulls her frayed skirt lower on her hips and saunters through the swaying grass like a panther.

Shuddering on Theresa's sagging porch, Dana looks up to her bedroom where a slight figure is silhouetted in the emerald–lit window. The figure, wrapped in a blanket, tentatively waves. Dana takes off Carl's hat, brandishes it over her head and tosses it into the jungle of the yard. She takes a cigarette out of her pocket and lights it. The nicotine clears her head, and she feels cleansed of her cop history. She has one last wild story to tell Ashley. "Once I was stupid enough to go alone to that cop bar on York Road," she says to the star–pocked sky, rehearsing. "There's no stopping some stuff, so don't go to reservoirs at night with strangers or into abandoned houses with a bunch of boys."

The light still flickers upstairs in Theresa's house.

The Whim of the
Great Magnet

I watch the Asian lady from my listing, enclosed porch. I had walked out to get the newspaper and the empty trashcan from the yard, but the sight of her stopped me. Across the street, she squats in front of my neighbor's yellow house, peering at a clump of weeds through a convex circle of something that looks like the lens of a magnifying glass or the face of a clock. The sparkling circle refracts rainbow rays in many directions. Some of it speckles her loose clothing; the lady wears tan sweat pants, house slippers, and a ruby, hooded jacket zipped against the heat of June. A floral, floppy hat hides most of her straight hair. She tilts her head as she examines the weed leaves and sketches an invisible pattern in the air with her bare hands with the grace of Tai Chi.

An oblivious white man with frizzy hair leads a brown standard poodle past my neighbor's house, and the dog sniffs at the crouched woman, whimpers and moves on. Steadying the glass, the Asian lady tentatively pats the vegetation.

I've seen her before.

Last week, when Cold Henry took me to dinner, she was looping circles outside Clementine Restaurant, her arms outstretched. Her right hand held a circle of light like the oval beam of a flashlight, but it pulsed as if she was channeling a moonbeam or signaling a star. Maybe she was studying the moon; it was full that night.

People walked around her. Cold Henry whispered something about the loco neighborhood of Hamilton, and I decided in that moment that I didn't want a third date with him. I believe that there's some sort of energy in the universe, some sort of magic. I can't name it, but I feel certain it can name me. I light candles and try not to lose my temper, but I haven't gone to church in years.

Inside the restaurant, Cold Henry dismissed the lady as insane. He believes only in mathematics. "Why speculate about crazy people?" he asked.

I push away Cold Henry thoughts; they take up too much time and energy.

I open the porch door; it creaks. The Asian lady doesn't flinch. I pause and head casually for the newspaper, whistling a few bars of Peter Gabriel's *Solsbury Hill*. The lady turns her head, but her shadow doesn't follow her to fall on the dandelion weed; it remains fixed. Luminescence springs from within her or shines through her. Somehow she seems more a part of this world than its chugging Gran Torino cars, racing dune buggies, and skateboarding teens, as if the forsythia bushes heavy with honeysuckle had produced her.

She seems to have weight. I wonder if she's real. Some ghosts seem real, I think. Maybe she's why my clocks have been running down lately.

Suddenly, I smell electricity from across the street, mixed with scent of ozone, like a wet street after a light rain. I'm envious of her single-mindedness; I have a hard time concentrating for very long before I have to find an excuse to go to the bathroom, refresh my coffee, or throw in a load of laundry. Concentrating is so exhausting, and I need breaks. Somehow, though, time has passed, and this woman continues to focus on the weeds so intently they seem to respond to her, to stretch up toward her, extending, and growing.

It's still Saturday on my front yard where I hold the newspaper in my hands, staring. The mailman saunters by, bag swinging. I mutter hello, and he returns my greeting. He gives the lady a wide berth, walking in a wavering loop around her. He's a stocky fellow with a fine halo of thin hair.

He saw her. The dog smelled her. Cold Henry saw her.

Somehow, I taste a drop in barometric pressure, metallic and sugary. I wonder if I've tapped into some ancient awareness buried somewhere deep within my lizard brain. I fear that reality is not a long train of moments all strung in a row like the subway; it circles around and makes me dizzy. I'm afraid to speak; I fear I might wake her into this particular reality. In waking the lady, the universe might tilt and fall to its side. I never felt this power before, and the responsibility of it is daunting. I've never had these thoughts before; I don't know their source.

Still, she studies the weed.

It's my property, at least a third of it. (The bank temporarily holds the other two thirds in my thirty–year mortgage.) I sit on the curb and tuck the newspaper plastic wrapper under my leg. The front page seems weirdly to be reported from a series of different time periods. *The Orioles win the World Series. The Baltimore Development Corporation demolishes the Mechanic Theatre. President shot. Hamilton man finds bleeding woman on his lawn in the middle of the night.* Baffled, I lower the paper. The lady has vanished. I stand and look up and down the street, the pages falling from my hands and the wrapper flying down Roselawn Avenue. Someone mows a lawn further up the hill. Someone yells out a window to a husband in his truck. Someone climbs a tree. Someone gardens. The trash truck trundles by. It's oddly soothing. I fit into the Hamilton air like a fish fits in water. It holds me in place. The valley fits the sky.

I gather the newspaper and pull my empty trashcan around the side of my house where I find the lady lying on her stomach in my backyard, like she has always been there, studying the mass of mint that grows through my slatted fence. I stand rooted with the can; I release its handle.

I feel compelled to speak, now that I am in another part of the yard, although I don't know why that matters. I mean to say hello, but instead I announce that I am indigenous as if I was answering the queries of a social anthropologist. "The salt on my skin seasons the night," I say, stringing together words that I usually don't string together. She nods or maybe the yard leans. "I don't know what that means," I admit.

She sniffs. The forest of mint perfumes the wind, weaving a saccharine baby's breath, moist and bubbling. The light is dappled and vaguely pale green as if the mint towered over me.

Mad thoughts swamp my mind, drowning logic. Like the camera obscura, the world's upside down and backwards, and all the maps are the wrong shape. Maps should include energy meridians, like ley lines, the magnetic strips that wrap the globe. The lady must know where they vibrate. Some ley lines must bisect my yard; my garage door malfunctions depending where I stand with the clicker. The mysterious forces of the earth ultimately destroy all of my electrical equipment, deceptively tugging metal shavings across the floor of my compass skull, reversing the charges, and mystically re–building the patterns.

I need a Rosetta Stone to process this experience. I've never considered the magnetic characteristics of my head or my property. I begin to count to ground myself. The numbers screech: seven tulips; fifty rusted peach Formstone squares; thirty-two blue gray ones; twenty daffodils; four hundred roof tiles; eighty grape hyacinth; one hundred fence slats; ten thousand blades of grass; and millions of ants and spiders. I can't look into the tangle of the forsythia; there are too many petals.

The lady rolls over onto her back and blows up at the clouds, her cheeks puff. A storm advances. A few drops of water sprinkle. Three buffalo–shaped clouds sprint by; time gallops faster. Maybe she's flutterng the eastern edge of this agreed–upon perception or somehow her breath is impacting the headlines in the paper under my arm.

"Are you decoding ancient messages?" I ask, stepping carefully toward her, like I was approaching a ticking bomb. "Am I standing in the right place in the mint?" I try to make sense.

She focuses on me, like a laser, her black eyes flashing. The sun seems brighter or else a cloud shifts. My mouth opens. My neurons and blood cells wobble. My capillary beds fill. My outer skin cells warm and tan.

The lady holds up the lens and two–dimensional images are instantly projected into my backyard.

Although I don't know the exact age of my house, suddenly I see it a hundred years ago in its framed shape and hear workers yell and hammers ring. They don't use electrical tools, and they're in period dress. Then that image slides to the right like a photo on my smart phone. One hundred and fifty years ago, the house is gone. A Confederate scout hides under the backyard brambles from Major General George Sykes' division as they march north to Gettysburg. I smell sharp fear and hear the crackle of the Union horses stepping on branches down the woods that is to be Roselawn Avenue. Two hundred years ago, a sheep gives birth in the backyard under a gathering of apple trees; a shepherd calls, and his charges bleat in return.

Three hundred years ago, an Iroquois hunting party stalks a deer; they make no noise. Four hundred years ago, a snake swallows a rabbit, like the creation of the earth. Five hundred years ago, a squaw builds a fire in the woodland clearing; I hear the click of her stones. Six hundred years ago, the land floods. Seven hundred years ago, a beaver looks for Herring Run creek. Eight hundred years ago, the bees own the glen; they buzz around a circle of stone obelisks that point toward Orion's Belt. More time rolls, and dinosaurs eat giant tree ferns.

I close my eyes and see those flashing eye lights inside, vibrating strings in a field of massing black, expanding in the center until two strings tremble inside that circle, dark and crossed like chromosomes.

I open my eyes, and my house is covered with vines. The sky is purple and braided with lightning, and a pack of dogs silently lope by.

I cover my face and sit on the moss of my yard. Pollen particles float by me like flurries, a manifestation of the true and hidden world. The Asian lady is gone again, along with her wild wormhole and my backyard portal to Orion's Belt. The air smells of electricity and mint. I feel my arms; they seem suddenly sun–burnt. I think I hear the giddy hum of the Great One priming the angle of the poles.

"Did you see a woman with a big floppy hat and a piece of glass?" I ask an old man walking down Hamlet Avenue. I'm surprised I can speak.

He is tall and patrician with hawk–like features. He's wearing a dark trench coat, although it's muggy outside. He turns his bald head and stares at me. He smiles the smallest of grins and nods, and I know at once that I am one of his numbered, but he hasn't come for me on this day.

"I think it's Saturday," he softly says.

It's still Saturday. This is now, I think: live in it.

Please do not enter.
This house was robbed
on April 20, 2011 and
four years before that.
It is picked clean; there
is nothing left to fence.
Really. I suggest
Worthington Valley or
Roland Park.

Special thanks:

Baltimore Fishbowl, Baltimore Sun, Joe Brady, J.J. Chrystal, Terri Ciofalo, Vicky Chiang, John Crowley, Skizz Cyzyk, Robert Daley (who produced *High Plains Drifter* with The Malpeso Co. and Universal Pictures), Jane Delury, Carlos Guillen, Hamilton Hills Neighborhood Association, the Hamilton Arts Collective, Harvest Fare Supermarket, Bill Henry, the Liquor Pump, Dave K., Kendra Kopelke, Susan Lynne, Stephen Matanle, Rain Pryor, Tony Reda, the Royal Farms Stores, David Simon, Lisa Tasker, Hunter S. Thompson, Pantea Amin Tofangchi, Joani Tompkins, Peter Toran, University of Baltimore, my whole class (especially Jacob Adams, Liz Bamford, Lauren Beck, Danielle Crawford, Jessica Jonas and Megan Stolz), John Waters, Joan Weber, and Gregg Wilhelm.

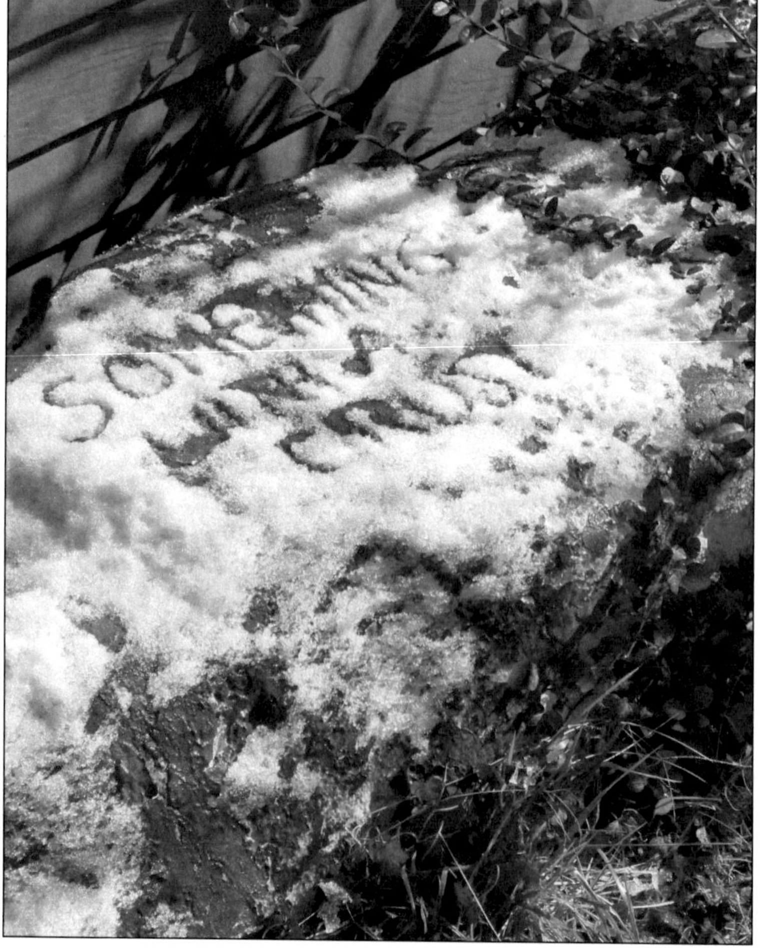

Colophon

Something with a Crust was designed by Kimberley Lynne in Gils Sans, Gil Sans MT and Perpetua typeface. All photographs were taken by Kimberley Lynne in Hamilton (except for Lake Montebello in contiguous Lauraville and the Liquor Pump in Parkville).

The cover image is Formstone. In 1937, Albert King of Baltimore patented Formstone, a stucco building application that gave the trompe l'oeil appearance of rock. Widely used in working class neighborhoods, Formstone was an art form; master Formstone artists imitated stone in design, coloring, and texture. In an interview in Skizz Cyzyk's documentary, *Little Castles,* film director John Waters described Formstone as "the ultimate. It's the polyester of brick."

In dreams, water is the symbol of change and emotion. Running Water Press tells stories, therefore, of emotional change.